ANARCHY IN NEW ENGLAND

JOE JARVIS

Joe Jarvis

Anarchy In New England

Joe Jarvis

FREE PRESS PUBLICATIONS

Published by Free Press Publications
http://FPP.cc

ISBN: 1-9383571-9-1
ISBN 13: 978-1-938357-19-0

FREE PRESS PUBLICATIONS

Free Press Publications is an independent alternative media / publishing company, founded in June 2009, with the mission of "ensuring a FREE PRESS for the FREEDOM MOVEMENT" and to also give new authors an avenue for publishing freedom oriented material.

ONE

A window popped up, flashing red along the margins, on one of the three large screens surrounding the operator. She was seated at one of the control panels on the top floor of New England Security Agency headquarters.

"Control to units, respond: 453 in progress at Riverside Bank, Worcester region, 1725 Atlantis Ave." She calmly spoke into her headset after activating the proper channel.

"Ground unit NESA21pv two kilometers north, in transit," immediately came the first reply, as a blue circle began blinking on an electronic map on the control panel. The light quickly halted, and reversed direction.

"Pv unit in transit," the operator repeated back, requesting air support, please respond."

"Air unit AP17a 4.8 kilometers southwest, in transit. Will drop tactical response unit AP3t at scene." This was a skyship unit from Atlas Protection responding to the call. A blue blinking triangle lit up on the map.

Another window popped up on the center screen at the operator station; this one showed overhead video from a satellite which had locked onto three men running down a street lined with buildings.

"Negative," The operator continued in her monotone voice, "Suspects fleeing south on foot down Sunset Lane. Establish visual before intervention. Two light skinned males, mid-twenties and early thirties, black clothing, one dark skinned male, black clothing, late twenties. At least two armed. All average height, average weight, one positive ID on facial recog, one tracker embedded, confirm signal."

"21pv confirming signal, in pursuit."

"Affirmative, 17a confirming signal, in transit, 2.2 kilometers south."

"453 at Riverside Bank, Worcester region, suspects fleeing south on Sunset Ave. Units in vicinity of Sunset mag-pod station respond," the operator relayed.

"NESA37pf .6 kilometers south on Sunset, in transit."

"Pf unit in transit, secure mag-pod station upon arrival. One suspect embedded with tracker, confirm signal."

"37pf confirming signal!" this time the response was not as dry, with heavy breathing. The two officers making up the foot patrol unit were running towards the station.

"21pv exiting vehicle, continuing pursuit on foot."

"17a has visual on two suspects, one light male with tracker, one dark male. Suspects turning, heading east on Cricket Ave."

"17a drop tactical unit AP3t 400 meters east of suspects, confirm drop," demanded the NESA operator.

It was about 20 seconds before the next update came into NESA headquarters from the air unit.

"17a confirming AP3t has repelled and is on the ground engaging suspects. Looks like 21pv is arriving on the scene. Suspects appear to be surrendering."

"Unit 21pv confirming, suspects have surrendered, and are subdued," the officer spat out between huffing and puffing.

The operator replied, in a tone that for the first time contained hints of enthusiasm, "A-ffirmitive. Good work. AP17a transport suspects to NESA processing center."

"17a confirming."

Another window popped up on the control panel, with flashing red borders. The operator transitioned seamlessly. She pressed a series of buttons to connect her to the proper channel.

"We have visual on third suspect of 453 at Riverside Bank, but no facial ID. Suspect is white, early thirties, wearing sunglasses. North Atlantic Clothing Group location 320 West Rock Street Worcester region, security cameras have suspect on surveillance, he appears to be attempting to blend in with shoppers. Units respond. Suspect may be armed."

"Ground unit MA112pf 500 meters west on West Rock Street, in transit." This time a foot patrol unit from Minutemen Arms responded to the operator.

"Pf unit in transit."

"Air unit MA54a 10 kilometers north, in transit."

"Air unit in transit, 112pf wait for MA54a before engaging suspect," the operator advised.

"Affirmative."

It was three minutes before the Minutemen Arms skyship arrived, and dropped their tactical response team.

"MA54a on scene, MA13t on ground. We have eyes on all exits to North Atlantic Clothing Group, in contact with 112pf."

"NESA dispatch confirming, proceed with engagement cautiously."

Another minute passed as the operator kept her eyes on the satellite video, streaming coverage from above the clothing store.

"MA13t has apprehended suspect without incident, will transport to NESA processing center via MA54a."

"Affirmative!" again, the operator's voice betrayed the slightest hint of enthusiasm. She concluded in monotone, "453 at Riverside Bank in Worcester region has been resolved, all units resume normal operations."

Mr. Drake sat at the head of the conference table mid-morning on Monday, the first day of fall. He looked like a bulldog ready for a nap. No one talked as his finger brushed from screen to screen on his tablet, thumbing through various reports from various offices of New England Security Agency. He read that for the second quarter in a row, NESA had barely broken even, squeezing quite minimal profits from the company that handled all kinds of personal security and investigation.

These meetings were awkward for Drake's management. To a certain extent their hands were tied, in all the wrong ways. Drake would insist on approving every single inter-company relation. This made NESA lose out on promising partnerships with other companies.

Drake, heavyset and medium height with a receding hairline, looked down over non-existent reading glasses. His head was tucked back so that his double chin blocked any sight of his actual neck. Everyone, not just his employees, addressed him as Mr. Drake, except a handful of friends who just called him Drake.

Drake looked back and forth between two executives, keeping his droopy eyes on each one for a few seconds. The younger of the two, a small dark male in his thirties called Jay was a public relations executive who had been with the company for 2 years, brought on in an attempt to transition NESA into a more modern economy. He was naturally energetic, and spoke up when he couldn't take the uncomfortable silence.

"I think that we should reach out to the Initiative for a Clean Environment and partner with them on a couple of basic services – nothing too elaborate!" he added, understanding full well the natural aversion Drake had to these sorts of collaborations. When he spoke his words seemed to bounce out of him. "But if you think about what people want these days, I mean, who is thinking about home invasions anymore? That's a thing of the past. People are more worried about pollution, clean air, clean water, sustainability. All we gotta do is give ICE members access to highway 90, to show we care. ICE tells their contributors and readers, and it creates some positive buzz. Word will spread, and maybe we get another opportunity to use 90 to our benefit. I mean, we're barely making anything off it now, we might as well use it as a bargaining piece, or get a little free advertising out of it."

Silence. It sounded to Drake like he would be giving away something for nothing. After all, if he didn't give away a few hundred thousand 90 passes to ICE contributors, some of them might use the highway anyway, and pay the toll. He wasn't sure it would drum up enough business to be worth it. Then again people only drove for fun these days anyway, preferring the magnet tunnels which sent pods zooming through above ground vacuum tubes, propelled by alternating electro magnets.

Drake didn't like the hassle. He was the type that just wanted to sell a product, and get money in return; he didn't understand why he always needed to be bothered with charity and business relations. He thought back fondly to the days when NESA was a customers' one stop shop for all their security needs.

"Alright Jay. Let's see if we can get some value out of that highway," Drake said, giving in. "Next order of business?"

"Sir, if you don't mind, I wanted to bring up the attempted bank robbery this morning at Riverside Bank," said the Vice President of Operations. Drake just looked up from his tablet at his VPO and waited. By now the VPO knew this meant to proceed.

"It was handled quite well, but I am concerned with the nature of the crime. This is the first attempted bank robbery in our area of coverage in..." he looked down at his tablet screen, "8 years. I don't think we should investigate this as an isolated incident, but rather as part of a possibly growing problem of cartels from New York City."

Drake's blood-hound eyes glanced around the room. "And how much would that cost?" he drawled slowly.

The VPO glanced at the Vice President of Finance, who chimed in, sounding bored, "We'd be looking at about 20% above normal costs," then he added as an afterthought, "but it could always save us money down the road."

"They're still at the processing center, is that correct?" Drake asked.

The VPO answered, "Yes, they are going to be transferred to confinement soon, to await arbitration."

"So their security companies didn't put up any fight?" the VPF added curiously.

"Only one of them even had representation; a company out in the New York City region. We sent them everything we had and they said it was fine to hold him. They're going to have an attorney contact one of ours so they can review the evidence. For the other one arbitration is going to let us know what they recommend for sentencing, if he is found guilty."

"Before you proceed with the larger scale investigation," Drake spoke slowly and deeply, his head tilted forward, so it seemed like he was looking down at everyone in the room, "Just check to see if they are in fact connected to any New York City cartels."

The VPO nodded.

The bored sounding VPF chimed in, "I thought there were three suspects?"

"Sorry..." the VPO interjected looking at his tablet concerned, with a furrowed brow, "It appears the third suspect never made it to the processing center. He was being transported by Minutemen Arms. The Atlas Protection skyship made the drop of the first two suspects, but the Minutemen Arms skyship never arrived at the processing center. It appears to have resumed normal operations and is back out on patrol."

Drake took a moment to respond, "Was the suspect embedded with a tracker?"

"No, we have that one in custody; he got tagged by the tracker at the bank when the alarm was tripped. For some reason we never got facial recognition on the missing suspect. Should I alert our dispatcher?"

"Hold on, hold on," Drake held up his hand, "Jay, what does the public know so far?"

"Nothing sir, other than that there was an attempted bank robbery, and we thwarted it."

Drake appeared to be deep in thought for some moments. "We have two suspects in custody. We don't even know where to start looking for this third guy: no tracker, identity unknown. No one was hurt... Let this one go, we'll prosecute the men we have in custody."

An awkward silence filled the room, and the executives were visibly uncomfortable; some stared at the table or blankly at their tablet screens.

Jay spoke up, "Sir, if the public found out..."

"It is *your* job, Jay, to make sure the public *does not* find out." Drake's dragon stare made eye contact impossible for Jay to maintain.

After some silence, the VPO timidly spoke up, "Should I inquire with Minutemen Arms how-"

"This issue is closed. Prosecute the two we have. Minutemen Arms will be just as happy not to be probed as to their transport failures. We needn't waste the resources. Anything else?" Drake asked, glancing around the room without moving his head.

"Yes sir," the younger voice of Jay spoke up again from further down the table, a bit timid, but still energetic. "You said you wanted me to bring by any new public relations representatives... so that you could make sure they understand how the company has evolved."

The seasoned executives braced themselves for a speech they had heard many times before, in one version or another. Drake made sure anyone new in management heard it from him: their jobs were owed to the selfless and tedious effort his family had exhorted in growing the company from nothing.

"Ah yes. Tell me..." Drake paused for a bit too long and the new executive in his 30's interjected nervously –

"Hunter."

Drake just looked at him almost confused. He hadn't paused to get the man's name, but rather to collect his own thoughts. After another pause where Drake pursed his lips and looked away to collect himself as Hunter's cheeks turned red, Drake continued: "Tell me, what do you know about New England Security Agency?"

The new hire launched into his knowledge of NESA, speaking a bit too quickly, swallowing and clearing his throat a little too often. "Uh, well, sir, uh, I know that New England Security Agency is one of the longest continuously operating personal security agencies in New England. I know it was, uh, started by your grandfather as a policing agency for people in the Worcester area almost, ahem, 70 years ago." Nervous swallow, clearing of the throat. "I believe I read that NESA first did work for a larger company, uh, Cape Cod Criminology who focused on investigation, mostly along the coast of the region."

The room became silent. "*Not bad*," Drake thought. He had certainly heard worse. While Drake's bulldog demeanor did not change, he nodded his head a few times in mild approval.

"Yes," Drake replied in a stately manner, "Cape Cod Criminology sold insurance to people who wanted protection, and my grandfather," Drake motioned to a portrait on the wall, without shifting his glance from Hunter, "provided a piece of that protection. He started small, mostly just with patrols and response, while Cape Cod Criminology would handle the investigation of crimes. Starting around here, close to the area where Food Corp opened its doors after the New Dark Ages, provided a large enough customer base so that the cost per customer was not overwhelming for a young up-and-comer like my grandfather. He had a reputation, you see, even before NESA was started. Everyone knew you could trust the man. It was only natural that he monetize that trust to keep people safer.

"My grandfather was one of the first police officers in the Worcester region after the 2020's collapse and 2040's rebound, and spent years accumulating enough capital to launch New England Security Agency. He had enough good relations in the security business to land the Cape Cod Criminology contract for the Worcester area as the company expanded west.

"At first, he handled patrols and emergency response for Cape Cod Criminology in most of central New England. NESA would check up on homes who subscribed to that service, and respond to emergency calls while on patrol. We were the first to enter into sharing agreements with other companies, so that we would respond to each other's customer in an emergency if we were closer, and settle up at the end of the month.

"This caught on quickly, and was soon adopted by every company in New England, setting the golden standard for security. We all have New England Security Agency, and my grandfather to thank for that. In fact we have him to thank for arbitration agencies as well, which younger folks might take for granted these days," Drake raised his eyebrows, staring almost accusingly at the younger men and women in the room. He had gotten to his feet and was slowly pacing around the large meeting table with his hands folded behind his back. Every now and then he would stop and make a hand gesture, or focus his stare at Hunter, who was sweating and nodding in agreement with wide eyes to every word Drake spoke.

"You see, not all security companies were as reputable as this one, back in those days. There was one who would not back down; protecting a vile man guilty of rape. All the evidence was against him, but the man had resources. It was our company against his company, and no agreement could be made. Well my grandfather, being a problem solver, got together with all his contacts from other reputable agencies, including Cape Cod Criminology, and started an association that would review cases, and hand down verdicts when two security companies could not come to an agreement. They called it an arbitration association, which eventually evolved into the arbitration agencies we have today. This system, now used the world over, has its roots in my family. Without my grandfather, who knows if rival agencies would still be battling to this day? Because of NESA, peace is a product in demand. And a valuable product at that!" with this Drake raised his index finger to accentuate the point.

"Think about the costs associated with war. Because of that arbitration association, we did not have to expend needless bullets, acquire expensive armor, build intricate fortifications, or expend human life. And yet we had an authority to review our data, and tell us when to allow action against a customer of ours – if they had violated another's rights. This way, we could offer the utmost protection, while not wasting resources defending guilty clients. The arbitration association notified security agencies of impending arrests of their clients, to allow for any appeals by the protecting agency, and so that agents would never draw guns on other agents. It was NESA who standardized cooperation among agencies, and legitimacy in criminal proceedings.

"And the trend my grandfather started concerning responding to others' customers, he also began in arresting suspects wanted by rival agencies. In hindsight it seems so simple, like bounty hunters of the old world, that a nominal fee is paid to the agency which captures the suspect. A simple idea, yet of no value until put to practical use.

"New England Security Agency expanded over the next 25 years to fulfill all contracts of Cape Cod Criminology. But when the time came to sign another exclusive contract, my grandfather, with the guidance of my father, negotiated a contract that kept all of NESA's prior duties under Cape Cod Criminology, but did not exclude the possibility of us fulfilling other contracts. This gave us room to expand, and with that, NESA opened our first insurance office, and began selling crime insurance, in addition to our policing activities.

"As my father took the reins of the company, business boomed, and New England Security Agency customers could be found from Bar Harbor to Hartford; from Burlington to Newport." Drake's back was now to his employees seated around the table, and he was staring at a large map of New England, mounted on the wall as he talked.

"By the time NESA reached 50 years as a company, it was New England's most successful and popular security agency. We boasted the lowest percentage of canceled contracts of any security agency in New England. Everyone knew we would go to bat ferociously for our truly innocent clients. But we were also respected for graciously abiding when one of our customers committed a crime. As our contracts still state, our protection will be withheld in the event that a customer commits a crime that has a clear victim. NESA's evidence has always been valued by arbiters because of its meticulous detail, and valued by customers because of the dedication we show in bringing criminals to justice, and protecting clients from wrongful prosecution.

"Fifty-three years after the company was founded, my father handed down control to me, and I became President and CEO." Drake turned back around rather quickly, remembering he was not alone in the meeting room. "And that is how this company came to be, and how it will remain. Working in public relations, it is up to you to keep the reputation of New England Security Agency as crystal clear as it was when my grandfather poured his blood, sweat, and tears into building it."

After a few moments of silence, with a continuous stare from Drake, Hunter realized it was his turn to respond. "I cherish the opportunity sir!" he quickly recovered.

Drake gave a final nod, and walked towards the conference room door. Before he left the room, Drake turned to add as an afterthought a brief closed mouth "smile" and eyebrow raise that quickly returned to a natural droopy face as he headed to his office.

The executives streamed out of the office in relief, loosening their collars and drawing deep breaths like they had just resurfaced from under water. Jay was filling in the blanks for Hunter.

"Drake has pretty much kept everything in the company the same for the past 15 years up to this point. Unfortunately, he's not always super accepting of new ideas... which makes us a little old school. Even though we still have some of the best numbers in New England, competition is rising to rival NESA. Really it's only been the last five years our region wide front runner status in the business has faded. Believe me, public relations is what this company needs now, more than ever."

Hunter was still nodding, but less nervous now. His head was spinning from having so much thrown at him all at once. As the two entered Jay's office and sat down, Jay continued.

"As profit margins shrank, Drake was forced to trim aspects of the company. Some of our investigations are now contracted out, and customer relations are handled by contractors more than ever before, which we, in part, oversee. There've been whispers that the company is in danger of shrinking back to its original state of little more than a patrol company. Essentially it's my job, and now yours, to make sure that doesn't happen. Sometimes it feels like we are swimming upstream, but it is really a rewarding job. Like today, Drake agreed to team up with ICE; that's a big step. I hope you're up for the challenge." Jay smiled at Hunter while taking a seat on the side of his desk with the drink he just poured.

"I'm excited to get started!" Hunter was relaxing a bit, but still seemed anxious. "Isn't it a little early to be drinking?" he questioned, adding a smirk when he realized the risk of offending Jay.

Jay laughed, and stood up to walk around his desk. "Its just after administration meetings that I pour myself a drink this early!" he joked. Jay swished around the remaining liquid in his glass, and downed the rest with a grimace. "What do you say I show you to your desk?"

Drake returned to his office to try to figure out how to keep the company profitable. Drake's office was furnished mostly in dark-stained wood with leather chairs, and bookshelves with books that looked like they were a hundred years old – some were. His desk sat in front of a large arched window reaching from just above the floor almost to the ceiling.

People were getting more bang for their buck these days from security agencies, and NESA customers had more than one reason to jump ship.

There was plenty of competition in the New England security market. Things were not very volatile, and crime was low, so there was not much risk to choosing cheaper options for security. People didn't often victimize others, at first because they knew they would get caught, but then out of habit. Everyone was raised to know that aggressing against someone was wrong, and there would be consequences. Additionally it seemed primitive to most people these days to use violence, or take something that didn't belong to them.

In New England, there was so much wealth, that no one would ever find themselves in the position where they needed to steal to survive, at any rate. Crimes of passion, though rarer, were the main form of deviance; but still, 1 murder per 100,000 people would be a year with a shockingly high rate.

Drake's failure was that he did not expand what his company offered in their security packages. Many security companies these days were smaller parts of larger insurance companies that did not only provide security, but offered trash pickup, fire protection, transportation, health insurance and a whole range of other services. Drake did not have the energy or business savvy of his grandfather or father, respectively. He was well-versed in economics, finances and accounting, but he was never that great in negotiations, and building relationships with other businesses. He was seen by other CEO's as a "my way or the highway" type guy, when the general business environment of the time was more flexible.

Businesses survived by working together. They survived by knowing their strengths, and recognizing their weaknesses. There was no shame in outsourcing an aspect of your company if it could be done better, and integrating products was in high demand throughout industries. For a population that all thrived on working together in their productive endeavors, these consumers demanded businesses that mirrored their needs, wants, and values.

Drake was too reluctant to make a deal with other highway owners when the bundling boom had most companies offering a one stop shop for multiple services. NESA owned highway 90 from Boston all the way to 20 miles east of Albany. But only NESA customers could get on without paying a toll every time they entered.

Drake was behind the times, because virtually every other highway in New England had ceased charging tolls years earlier. Instead highway owners made agreements amongst themselves to sell traveling rights to companies and customers in bundles. A Corner Cop Security sticker – embedded with a chip – gave access to just about every highway in New England, without making customers stop for a toll, because their toll was included in their Corner Cop Security package.

If an NESA customer wanted that kind of road access, they would have to purchase a separate travel package from another company. Vehicles traveling on roads without authorization were often issued citations and fines from patrolling officers; officers hired by the highway owner. They knew who had paid because the chip in the authorization stickers sent out a signal. And security companies often provided customers with a service that confirmed an officer stopping them was legitimate. But it was worth it to just get a travel package, not have to buy multiple road subscriptions, and avoid fees for traveling without a subscription. Customers liked when they could obtain multiple services through one company, it made things simpler when paying the bills.

And now, once again, Drake was looking at the all too familiar sight of slipping numbers, and customer cancellations. This is when Drake would normally cut another corner to save another buck, knowing full well he was just kicking the can down the road to the next quarter, when customer satisfaction would again fall, and he would be once again forced to find another dollar to cut from the budget.

Although a dollar didn't technically exist as a currency anymore, dollars were still referred to as units of measurement. One dollar could always buy the same amount of goods – a candy bar or a drink generally cost a dollar – but one unit of any particular currency might be worth ten cents, ten thousand dollars, or anywhere in between. Stores paid for a standardizing service at the checkout that told them how much to charge in any one currency, depending on the value at any given time, and their prices were expressed in dollars. Companies and banks were typically happy to have their currencies valued around $1 per unit.

Outside, the leaves were showing the first signs of change. It was that perfect crisp air that only required a sweatshirt to be comfortable. Drake momentarily let his mind wander to another fall day thirty years earlier when he wasn't holed up in his office. He was walking with a girl admiring the foliage, thinking that he could spend every day just like that one. She was smart, and always talked about becoming a teacher, but Drake would tell her she shouldn't stop there.

Drake quickly forced his mind back to business. He started to read the report on NESA's main competitors. Some companies were doing better this quarter, some worse, but none seemed to have much connection to NESA; about an equal number of customers left the other companies for NESA, and vice versa. There was no strong correlation between customers leaving for any other specific company, until he came across Atlas Protection in the report.

Atlas protection was a newer but established company which had recently been ramping up their services after a few years of extraordinary profits. In the previous 12 months, a whopping 22% of former NESA customers who canceled their policies had joined up with Atlas Protection. It appeared that most of them were saving money for basically the same service, and those that were spending more were getting more, a lot more.

Exit surveys identified the lack of additional benefits in security packages as the main reason for leaving, and it made sense that their destination would be Atlas Protection. An AP package gave you access to nearly every road and highway in New England – except route 90. But customers also cited AP's charitable giving as a reason for the switch. Every year 5% of all Atlas Protection profits were donated to various charities, so people felt like they were doing a good thing by patronizing AP, and they were.

Drake was glad that he had given the go-ahead to partner with ICE, but in his heart he knew it wouldn't be enough. He sat back and swiveled in his chair to gaze out the broad window behind him, thinking that there must be some way to rise again as a business. He had a primal urge for victory, and to crush his enemies in the dust, but a civilized society afforded no such opportunities. As Drake looked down at the street full of busy shoppers, and slow moving cars, he saw an all-black SUV with white letters emblazoned on the side that read, "Atlas Protection."

It was a busy day at Atlas headquarters; actually, every day was busy. The company was receiving an influx of new customers daily, and had been for some time. AP was successful originally because of the variety of package deals they offered for security. There were over a dozen plans to choose from, from a bare bones package to one with all the bells and whistles. And even then, it was easy for Atlas Protection customers to customize the plans for their needs.

A guy who lives off in the remote woods might only want legal protection in case he needs to call for an investigation. This type of crisis-only insurance was dirt cheap, and worth it since every company charged more for customers who only came to them after being victimized. Only a very small percentage of the population chose to purchase no security up front.

Other customers wanted the gold plan of multiple daily checkups of their property by AP officers. Obviously this was more expensive, and generally reserved for businesses, or the extremely wealthy. Sometimes neighborhoods would go in together for a patrol, and each household would purchase a separate more basic plan for their security needs. AP was happy to accommodate any customer, and the customers appreciated the excellent service.

Kittery Atlas was the President and CEO of AP, having started the company almost 20 years ago when he was only 35. Kittery, named after his birthplace, who went by Kitt, was medium height with mostly gray curly hair that would always get a little out of control before he cut it. In shape and energetic, Kitt's positive attitude infected his staff who swore they never saw the man have a bad day. That was probably because his home life was just as great as his office life. Happily married for 30 years, Kitt was the father of four, with two grandchildren, and a third on the way.

Kitt truly built the company himself from the ground up. For the first few years, his frugality was the only thing making the company survive. He hardly took a salary, and made sure to eat at his parents' house 2 or 3 times a week to save money. When Kitt was building his company he didn't have new clothes, he walked the 2 miles to work every day, and never drank alcohol – well, he never *bought* alcohol. Often a generous friend or family member would send a beer his way as a nice gesture.

But the days of want were over for Kitt and his family, though you might not know how profitable his company was by the way he lived. He and his wife kept the same modest home, though they made improvements and modernizations as the years went on. They had no need for luxury or expensive cars and clothes. Their one indulgence was vacations, often escaping from the grind 5 or 6 weeks each year to hit the best vacation spots on earth. As the years went on, Kitt added a vacation bonus for his employees, feeling guilty that they might not have the same opportunity to travel as he and his family.

Kitt's office door was never closed, and there was a near continual stream of employees filing in and out for various reasons. Kitt loved to be involved in the daily activities of the company, but was not a micro-manager. He generally listened to updates and said, "Okay, go get em!" with a genuine smile on his face. He was a great manager who didn't have to sacrifice morale for order. He could get the best employees because of his unmatched employment offers, and the lack of turnover further helped the company profit using experienced staff.

Over the past 5 years AP had really taken off, with so much growth it was tough to keep up. Kitt handled this by absorbing smaller companies, and introducing them to his business plan without shaking the place up too much. This meant he was not over-extended from expansion, and could gain new customers without them having to lose the old faces of their security companies. But once customers got a taste of patronizing AP, they were so impressed they told all their friends.

"Great job, can you send the Nashua branch manager a thank you for handling that issue so well?" Kitt was saying to a young female employee as he signed a tablet put in front of him by another, who swiftly exited with a nod. "It's great when we can avoid arbitration in small cases like that. Frankly I was surprised his security was even going to take it to arbitration. Thanks."

"Mr. Atlas," his secretary interjected, peeking her head around the door, "Molly Metis from Business Ethics Review is on hold."

"Oh! Thanks Jan," Kitt energetically replied, before turning to the young lady to whom he had been talking to finish, "Thanks, I gotta take this, let me know if he needs anything when you thank him!" He picked up the phone, "Hi Molly how are you doing on this fine fall day?"

"I'm great Mr. Atlas, and how are you? I just had a couple more questions that popped up for the article we're releasing next month on Atlas Protection."

"Absolutely, what have you got for me?"

Two

As Molly hung up she leaned back in her plush pink fluffy chair. She liked Kitt – good guy, always positive, charming really – not that it would have much influence on her article, AP *was* squeaky clean ethically. And what a contrast, she thought as she looked down at her next assignment; Mr. Barry, the arbitration agent. *Uhg!* She had dealt with him before, and getting a straight answer out of the man was like prying teeth. He always seemed to be hiding something, calculating, dodging. She couldn't quite understand his attitude since she had never uncovered anything *too* unsavory about Barry Arbitration – just that he hired a few family members who might have not been *completely* qualified for their position. But after the Business Ethics Review (BER) report, they were all given lucrative severance packages, and sent on their way. Barry's reputation didn't suffer too much from that slip up, since he acted quickly to remedy it.

Molly was in her early thirties, had tan skin (even in the New England winter), but bright blue eyes – which was rare as the recessive trait was quickly disappearing in the modern worldwide melting pot. Molly's nose was small and sharp, but the rest of her facial features were more rounded. Her hair was wavy and light, almost too blonde for her skin tone; but it was natural, and looked natural. She was a stunning woman by anyone's standards; not a stick figure but certainly not chubby either.

People that were too skinny were found unattractive in 2115, because it wasn't too long before that this signified starvation, disease, and death. Weight was actually more moderate than before the collapse. Very few people were obese, because the market had geared towards less meat and oil consumption after the collapse, and healthier, leaner food options in general. But with the collapse fresh in the collective memory, people saw the benefit of having a little extra in case things went sour. Nuts remained a favorite source of protein, keeping well without refrigeration or salting (unlike meat). Diets were extremely varied, since food could be shipped quickly anywhere around the globe and remain fresh. An orange picked on the Florida peninsula in the morning could easily be eaten by an urban New Englander that same afternoon. This also meant fewer preservatives were necessary, so natural farming stayed the standard even in the Modern Renaissance.

Lots of bad habits of food production were lost after the collapse, and as populations rebounded, the market provided the means for agriculture to remain natural, with the example set decades earlier by Food Corp, the miniature walled city that survived the 2020's collapse of society by building skyscraper farms and factories centered in what was then called Massachusetts.

Barry had left four questions blank on a recent survey for BER, and the survey itself he had been returned late. Molly mustered the energy to make the call to Barry. She flicked on her video screen, and pressed Barry's number.

"I told you I don't want any calls right now!" snapped Mr. Barry to his secretary. He was his typical, uneasy self that morning. He hated talking on the phone, and dealing with customers, except for a few of his favorites. But even then he was more interested in playing golf, or attending dinner parties than conducting business. His reputation as an arbiter had slowly diminished over the years so that many of his clients were slightly less than reputable these days.

Rumors had swirled now for a few months that Mr. Barry had taken a bribe to ignore a breach of contract one of his customers committed against their colleague. This was being investigated by Molly from Business Ethics Review, who Mr. Barry was already on shaky terms with for being standoffish and failing to disclose records pretty much every arbitration agency gladly shared with reputable publications like BER. Most of the remaining honest customers left the agency as soon as they learned of Barry's lack of cooperation, but a BER finding of corruption would essentially doom the company – it would be bankrupt in a matter of months.

"It's Molly from BER," shot back his secretary, not quite rude, but obviously annoyed at Barry's demeanor. The secretary was used to Barry's attitude. She was reminiscent of a 20th century librarian, with a tight graying bun and seeming to wear invisible glasses which she would look over when she wanted to talk down to someone in the waiting room. She took liberty to talk back to Barry because through the years she had deleted a number of sensitive documents, and erased a number of sensitive files, and made a number of sensitive calls on Barry's behalf. She had job security as long as Barry Arbitration existed.

"God damn it." Mr. Barry looked at the screen as if trying to figure out some way to dodge the call. His lips curved into a frown as he reached for the screen, then hesitated, cleared his throat, and quickly hit the "receive" button, the motion of his hand invoking images of a striking snake. Most people used the two way screens when answering calls, but Barry habitually disabled his camera.

"Hello Ms. Metis so good to hear from you!" Barry said a bit too joyfully and a little too loudly. But he wasn't fooling anyone, especially not Molly, with his fake enthusiasm.

"Hi... Mr. Barry" Molly stumbled a bit when Barry's screen remained black instead of his face popping up as with most people on a call.

"How can I best serve you today Molly – may I call you Molly?" Barry wasn't letting up on his happy-go-lucky act.

"That's fine." Molly said shortly. "I am just calling to find out why you left four questions blank on the survey that you returned to us last week."

"Oh did I? An oversight I'm sure."

"Well that's what you said the first time, but you still failed to fill out the information when we resent the form."

"Just message that over to me and I'll..."

"Frankly we need to clear this up in person, BER has a policy that a personal interview is required if it is determined that the subject is refusing to answer certain questions."

"I'm insulted!" Mr. Barry retorted unconvincingly – he was well aware of this policy. "I am certainly not trying to be evasive, why don't you come by next Tuesday."

"Tomorrow or Thursday would work much better for me. It will be almost as bad for your company to have a blank rating when the report comes out next month than to get a C rating... assuming you answer my questions to BER's satisfaction."

Barry hesitated, as if again attempting to think of an exit plan. With a slight sigh that he hoped Molly did not detect, Barry replied, more subdued than before, "Ah, Thursday will be fine. Come by after lunch."

"Thank you Mr. Barry, I will see you around 13:00," responded Molly before she hung up.

Barry's fake smile (which he was wearing despite disabling the video screen) quickly vanished as he hit the "end call" button.

Frown returning, Barry ground his teeth, reaching for the scotch bottle in his top drawer – it was already half empty. Barry was in his mid sixties with gray hair that slightly receded away from his forehead. He had a matching gray goatee that formed a small triangle; Barry must have used gel or wax to keep it in place, and sometimes when he would twist it out of habit, the goatee would develop some curls. He was bony and pale with red cheeks, and bags under his dark blue eyes; the iris sometimes blended right in with the black of his pupils. His ears came to dull points at the top, and extended to the sides a bit further than normal. His nose was slightly rounded, and his lips were thin.

Barry was old enough to remember as a child, politicians. He was envious of the lost profession, and wished he could have lived in a time where he didn't have to spend every day fighting his competitors to stay in business.

"*It is too much work! Haven't I earned enough already? It is a cruel society that forces an aging man to work his fingers to the bone everyday just to turn a profit. It is pathetic,*" he thought as he swigged his scotch from an iceless glass like a pirate drinking rum, *"that I have to attend charity events in order to make speeches and take my rightful place at the head of a crowd. Government events would provide me a much more fitting platform"*, but the days of government in New England were a distant memory.

Even the politicians that Barry remembered were hardly the type that used to inhabit every region of the continent and globe. The politicians from Barry's childhood were mayors and local selectmen who were big fish in a small pond. In the end they were out-competed by bigger, private entities which delivered all the benefits of a town government, for a lower cost, and without compulsion.

It was the force that Barry envied most. As an arbiter he was well aware of having to negotiate and concede; having to finely word agreements so that he could squeeze a little gain out of hours of hard work. He wished more than anything that he could simply issue a proclamation, and have that be law!

Law: a dead meaning really, the word more applicable in the modern day to scientific principles. What was once called law was now called agreements, contracts, and free association. What was even more aggravating to Barry was that for every little litigation he had to find a victim. How many times had the perfect opportunity arisen to help along a business he had invested in – by ruling against a competitor – only to lack a victim! In the good old days, it could be claimed that society in general was the victim.

Money had only gotten Barry so far, and although he had plenty, it would not support him at his current spending habits for thirty years of retirement. And given the choice between money and power, Barry would have taken power any day, if true power was still available; power in the old sense of the word, where people in the right positions could do whatever they wanted without retaliation. But power was no longer derived from who had the most guns and the biggest muscles. Today, power flowed to those with the most friends, who had helped the most people, who never tired of positive interactions and good intentions. They had influence; the power of networks, the power of acquaintances. Barry knew all too well the detriment of burning bridges. His company could have been the largest in New England if not for an event, 30 or 40 years earlier.

Mr. Barry read a lot of books and boasted an antique library in his home full of novels and texts from before the collapse. He still enjoyed paper pages, and had as much interest in historical works as he did in old fiction from the 20th century. He read about when there were governments, and he pined to have an agency at his disposal like the FBI, daydreaming about standing in J. Edgar Hoover's shoes. He read about how the FBI once raided the lab of a guy named Tesla, just because a rich tycoon, JP Morgan, told them to do so. He read about hits carried out by the CIA on reporters and loudmouths who threatened the power structure of politicians and bureaucrats. He poured over books about judges giving decades long sentences to rape victims for "perjury", and other judges giving time-served to their rapist friends. He slipped into a daydream about having the power of force at his fingertips.

He thought about Molly driving home from work, hitting the brakes and nothing happening. He thought about her frantic expression, her terrified scream, and her car burning all around her. Barry imagined Molly walking down the sidewalk to work, with a coffee in one hand and a tablet in the other when, BOOM, a bullet slams into her skull and out the other side, spraying brains all over the sidewalk and onto the wall behind her. Finally Mr. Barry could not help but let a real, genuine smile cross his lips.

"Ahh..." he sighed. If only things were as easy for people like him as they used to be. *But why can't they be again?* It was wishful thinking. And Barry knew he was dreaming if he thought he could get away with killing a reporter. The investigation would inevitably lead back to him if he hired anyone to do it, and every cent of his money wouldn't be enough to pay off a single security agency, let alone the dozen that would be involved in one way or another with the investigation.

The frown had returned to Barry's face because he knew there was nothing he could do to stop the corruption report from surfacing. But he had to do *something* to avoid the impending report ruining his business. Security agencies and their customers would be furious, and the last thing he wanted was protesters outside the building; the quickest way to make customers drop like flies. And once customers started leaving an arbitration agency it was doomed to the snowball effect. He would be forced out of business, and worst of all start burning through his savings. Unless Mr. Barry wanted to be doomed to a retirement of playing golf at pay-per-game courses and drinking merely $90 per bottle scotch he had to do something. But what to do, that was the problem!

"Well I'm not going to get any work done with myself all in a frenzy like this!" he thought to himself, and he got up to head out to lunch at Hillside. At least at Hillside he could consort with the movers and the shakers, and forget his current problems. There's nothing like a $500 lunch to clear the mind!

On his way out of the building Mr. Barry saw a familiar and unwelcome face at the bottom of the steps to the sidewalk. It was the drug addict, Trix, who would make rounds a couple times a week in this part of town, because he could always manage to squeeze a few bucks out of the folks who found it worth it to slip him a few dollars in exchange for leaving them alone.

"I just need $5 to get back uptown," Trix said to Barry as he descended the stairs.

"Like hell," Mr. Barry thought to himself as he prepared to ignore Trix and brush past him, possibly hurling a witty insult at him... if he could think of one in time. But just as he opened his mouth to snarl something nasty at Trix, a client yelled his name from a half block down the sidewalk.

"Mr. Barry! How are you? Leaving early to enjoy the fresh air?"

Uhg. It was one of those good customers who barely cost him a dime or a minute of time, just paid to have an arbiter on retainer for his businesses. He had to be nice to him, it would be too easy to patronize someone else, and Barry knew the only reason he stayed with BA was that he had been with them for two decades. They always saw each other at the charity events, so the client wrongly assumed Barry to be considerate of his fellow man.

"Oh, hello!" Mr. Barry greeted the client with the same fake smile he wore on the call with Molly. "And here you are young man. Get yourself something to eat," Barry continued, handing Trix a dollar, hoping his client would mistake it for $5.

"Thanks," Trix said without expression, looking disappointed with the amount in his hand, as he walked away down the sidewalk, but Barry had misjudged his client.

"You know, you shouldn't give those types money, nope, they'll just use it on drugs, you know? It's better to walk with them to a shop and get them a sandwich or something. Actually..." the client dug in his pocket, "I know you'll be interested in this, being the charitable guy you are. Here's a card for my new project. I'm working with a couple of advertisers to promote a clinic that helps people kick their drug habits," he handed Barry a card. "If you just call this number you can donate money in someone's name that will go towards their treatment if they show up, then the ball's in their court, you know? If they don't go for treatment within a couple months, it helps someone else. But I'm sure you'll see him again, that's the one they call Trix isn't he?"

"Uh, yes, I believe so..."

"Well then you can let him know next time. He's somewhat of a regular around here, right? Doesn't hurt anyone, but it's still sad to see young people killing themselves like that. Anyway I've got to run, business to attend to, you know how it is. Enjoy this weather!"

"Ah yes, I will... and uh, thanks for the..." Barry looked at the card in his hand and turned it over and back ."..card." He nodded and flashed an extra closed mouth smile to make up for the hesitation.

"You bet!"

Mr. Barry made sure his client had turned the corner before he threw the card in the trash. As if he would waste money on some dope fiend when he had his own problems to deal with. He again daydreamed of the governments he knew from books, that would simply lock up those type in jail for doing drugs.

Everyone in society would chip in to pay for it, and it kept most of these areas sanitized! If the addicts weren't in jail, they were in the ghetto where they belonged, not living side by side with honest hard working people! But with all this extra wealth floating around these scum had options in this society.

"*How ridiculous,*" thought Barry, "*that I have to demean myself laboring day in and day out for my money, while Trix just begs and collects free handouts on every corner. Pathetic.*"

Barry waved his mini-tab at the receiver on the magnet tunnel terminal to order a level 1 pod to pick him up. It was there in a matter of seconds, and when the door slid open, Barry could see that it was sparkling clean unlike the level 2 or, God forbid, having to take a level 3 pod!

These reverse magnet tunnels were vacuum sealed and shot pods – compact cylindrical capsules where up to ten people or cargo was carried – through the mostly above ground tubes which ran along highway medians, roads, old railways and the like. Drop off points were mostly terminals owned by various pod companies, though hospitals, security companies, and big businesses, as well as some extremely wealthy people had the tube built right into their buildings or houses. A few people had their own pod, but mostly everyone just ordered them at the terminal, and the closest pod in the quality level selected would come, unless you saved preferences for pod companies. Riders could use or refuse specific pod companies, but this could make the wait up to ten minutes if the closest vacant pod was 400 or so kilometers away.

Pods traveled through the magnet tunnels at up to 5000 kilometers per hour, with vast tube networks running all across North America, and into other parts of the world. There was no air resistance or friction inside the tubes to slow them down. A few major pod tunnel companies had built the largest and most central veins of the system where pods going long distances would get up to top speed. But the smaller tubes with less traffic capacity and more turns would go slower. The system was all automated and in order for a company to plug in, their system would have to be compatible with whatever company owned the tunnel at the point where the new connection would be made. That company already had to make theirs compatible to plug in, and so forth.

The telescreen was running a news broadcast when Barry entered his pod. It was Crystal Carriers pod company who owned this particular news agency and automatically set the channel to their news station in all their pods.

"The independent pod system in Texas, continues to be plagued by safety hazards, while costs and customer prices remain above those for mag pods within the New England Style Economy," a women's soft therapeutic voice explained. "Although the state of Texas regulates the system's safety standards, another accident occurred yesterday when two pods collided. All 11 occupants were killed when a safety feature failed, propelling a pod into an occupied tunnel at 1200 kilometers per hour where it rear-ended another pod that had slowed to 500 kilometers per hour for a curve.

"This is the second major magnet pod accident in Texas since 2113. An investigation into that previous accident revealed that a Texas government official was bribed to look the other way on the safety features in the code, while the public assumed there was no risk to the system. The company originally contracted to build the system had donated to over 50% of Texas's statewide politicians, sparking accusations of political influence in selecting the contractor. Texas' independent system does not use the same technology and coding as the worldwide New England System, which is why they have yet to plug in.

"To contrast the safety of the Texas magnet tunnel system with that of the New England Style Economy system, the worst accident on record killed 9 people in 2 pods when a safety backup procedure failed. The code was rewritten, the victims' families given a generous reparation by the company, and the CEO took to traveling in her mag tunnels very publicly with her family to alleviate fear of another crash. That was Tunnel Cake CEO Athena Driver, and happened 23 years ago this December. Since then, only six accidents have occurred in the entire New England system, leading to fewer than a dozen casualties, making the New England Style Economy magnet tunnel pod system the fastest and safest way to travel, in the history of the world.

"The Crystal Carrier that you are traveling in – " Barry pressed a button on the armrest that switched the telescreen to a crackling fire. He let out a relaxed sigh as he sat back on the extra plush seat cushion and closed his eyes, whizzing off towards Hillside in the magnet tunnel.

Trix kept walking. He planned on taking the conveyor 17 blocks up town, but he needed the dollar Barry gave him in order to get an entire gram. Trix was a young adult, a bit too skinny with slightly sunken cheeks and set-back eyes with shadows underneath, and a tendency to slouch. His skin was paler than natural, and blue veins showed through in a few noticeable spots on his face. His natural hair color was black, though he had bleached it a month back. The roots were showing dark now, and his hair which grew straight up was leaning over due to its length, starting to cover his ears. His clothes were casual, too baggy, but not ragged, left over from when he filled them out, before the drugs had changed his look.

Many roads in the most populated areas had been restricted to walking, biking, and conveyors by the owners of the roads. Moving conveyor belts were built into some streets, set up in parallel rows of 3-6, each about one meter wide and traveling at a slightly higher speed than the adjacent belt. Pedestrians would access them through a gate with subscription or single payment options. Then they would step onto the first conveyor which traveled at a speed of about 5 kilometers per hour, with each parallel conveyor increasing by about 5 kph. In a 4 conveyor system, the furthest conveyor would travel at about 20 kilometers per hour, and a pedestrian would walk across the three slower moving belts in order to get to top speed.

Connecting belts traveled at the slowest speed when riders needed to take a turn or divert in order to get to their destination. Most systems were made up of several miles of conveyors in the most densely populated areas of cities, or sometimes only a one or two mile loop placed downtown. This particular area had a vast conveyor system which would reach most parts of the city. In New England no official cities existed in terms of government, but people still referred to where they lived by town, city, or region, which designated no more than a geographic area.

Trix had managed to scrape together $10 (in various currencies) that morning from begging, and found another $2 on the ground. He earned $3 picking up coffees for some businessmen who were working outside of their building. If he covered Jim's store for half an hour while Jim took a break he would get another $4, and that would get him a gram. Jim owned a small drug distribution store in the worst section of town – which was only four blocks.

The same vacuum tube system that shuttled people all over the world hosted smaller magnet tunnels to ship goods. Most shopping was done from home, and many items were shipped on the spot and arrived just seconds after ordering. Jim sold drugs from his distribution center, packaging them as the orders came in online, and shipping through the small mag pod port that hosted pods the size of basketballs. But next to that port was a tube that hosted larger pods: spheres with a diameter of about 1.5 meters.

There were multiple size shipping tubes, and not everyone had them built into their homes. It was relatively inexpensive to have a small tube installed, but many centers existed that hosted larger tubes, and charged a fee for anyone who wished to ship something there to be picked up. Of course there were also store fronts that specialized in letting people see, feel, and try out products before they were sold. But Jim got orders on his website from all over the world, though his business was still small. For that reason, he also served as a shipping center where people could pick up their larger goods. The bigger the tubes, the more expensive it was to have them built into your building.

"Did you eat anything today?" Jim asked Trix when he arrived at the store a half hour later.

"Yea they were giving away some new, like, burrito thing downtown."

"What are you going to have for dinner?"

"Do we have to go through this every day?"

"Do you have to get high every day?"

"You're the one selling it to me."

Jim frowned. "Look, I only ask because I care. The church on Oak St. has a free dinner every Monday and Thursday, you should stop by."

"I'll be fine, I get enough to eat, man."

"Yea but you don't get the nutrients you need! All I see you eating is crap."

Trix was done with the small talk. "Do you need a break? Let me stock some pods for a half hour."

Jim looked down sighing, "Alright," he said shaking his head a bit, "I'll be back in 30."

There was no real risk leaving Trix in charge of his store for a half hour. Jim had the security, and he knew Trix just wanted to get his fix. Stealing would mean time in confinement, without easy access to any drugs, and Trix was well aware.

When the half hour was over Trix took his gram and walked the block to his apartment.

It was an advertisers' apartment commonly referred to as an adap. Free room, free water, free electricity, free heat: the only catch was that the walls were covered in advertisements for all sorts of products, most of which were sold in the store that filled the wide hallways at the entrance and exit of the building, or could be shipped directly to the apartment via small shipping mag pods.

Pretty much anyone could get a free adap, but Trix was at the bottom rung, ranked a low priority consumer because he hardly bought anything. Still, it was worth it for advertising companies to keep these apartments; the advertising was so targeted that somewhere around 97% of adaps proved profitable according to various studies. And anytime an adap tried to kick out someone who wasn't buying anything, the public backlash was a greater threat to their profits than the few people gaming the system.

The apartments ranged in size and style. Even some very wealthy folks would get a penthouse adap at the top of the buildings where the advertisements were for luxury goods, services, and travel. But Trix's adap was on the sleazier side due to its location. Adap dwellers had to spend a certain amount of time at home to keep it, but it amounted to little more than half the year, meaning those who traveled for work would use an adap sometimes instead of hotels. Other people were just extreme couponers, and loved to get good value. Some college kids would get an adap to save money, or single moms so that they could be home for their kids. Trix had his because he liked to spend what little money he could gather on drugs.

He opened the door to his 2nd floor studio adap and the wall screens flickered on. A mild voice greeted him by name, asking if he had given much thought to skin care lately, and maybe he needed some help clearing off the blemishes on his face. He hit the "off" button on the wall panel, which made the room go silent, though the walls still offered information on a dozen products at least.

Every couple of minutes one of the panels would switch to another advertisement, but generally only one wall contained video advertising. Trix's whole apartment was seven meters long by six meters wide, with a three by four meter section on the right of the entrance for a bathroom and closet. The three meter section beyond the bathroom had a basic kitchenette. The rest of his adap was pretty bare. Trix had a mattress with some sheets, a coffee table, and a TV. His kitchen was dirty with all of the few plates, pots, and pans he owned piled in the sink, as they had been for months. The trash emitted a fishy odor, and overflowed with takeout boxes, and wrappers left over from weeks of being ignored. Every couple of months Trix would find a day of inspiration, clean his adap – well, his version of clean – and look into getting a job, or rejoining UtopaCorp. It usually lasted until about 16:00 when he would break down and go to buy or find more drugs. He had been a daily user for less than two years.

At 18 Trix went to work for UtopaCorp since he didn't have many other options. UtopaCorp was one of a few companies that would offer a job to practically anyone who wanted a job, and would follow UtopaCorp's rules. Usually it was "hippies," or people who wanted to party, who couldn't organize their lives, or young folks who didn't have many friends or family that joined up. The company would offer low take home pay, but take care of every aspect of their employees' life. Apartments were included, and the advertising stayed in the halls so employees could relax without products being shoved in their faces. Meal plans were included for all employees, and a plethora of sports, clubs, and activities were planned by employee groups for down time and weekends. They worked more hours than most people – about 40 each week – but the jobs were generally easy, and employees had no stresses of paying bills, or worrying about...well, anything really.

UtopaCorp placed workers in one of their many roles, top-heavy towards manual labor and low skill jobs. The company would offer all sorts of contracts that made sense for different people. Some employees had practically no access to their wages, as specified by the original contract they signed, instead placing the pay into high-interest accounts to earn money and help them control their spending. Others would take all their money up front.

UtopaCorp was willing to structure employment in a way that worked for the individual, as long as they showed up when you were supposed to, and did the job required. Trix lasted a little over two years with the company before he couldn't handle the structure anymore, and quit. He traveled with the money he had saved up until that ran out eight months later, at which point he had already formed some bad habits from some of the people he chose to associate with. It was another year before Trix was unable to hold a job for more than three weeks, and that is when he became a daily drug user. Trix knew his 25th birthday was looming, and it depressed him.

He thought about how unfair it was that he was stuck in some crummy adap while so many in the world had so much. He felt sorry for himself that during his traveling days he could only afford level 3 pods while he watched snobby college kids grab a level 1 with their daddy's credit. He heard you could order drinks in the level 1 pods, and they would pop up cold and fresh from the storage compartment below, but he had never been in a level 1 pod.

As Trix injected half a gram into his arm with an EZ-Ject syringe (which also appeared in an advertisement on the wall a few feet away), he fell into a nirvana like daze of imagining his life if he were rich.

Half dreaming, he imagined what it would be like to get a nano-bot injection of immune boosters that eliminate 97% of disease before the host even notices them, never having to feel sick, never having to wait two weeks to get rid of scabies with the topical ointment from the free clinic. He pictured himself taking a trip to a moon resort, driving the rovers over craters, and laying in a lounge chair under the glass dome, being waited on, while gazing at the earth from a perspective he would never know. Trix wanted to eat at Hillside, and be invited to a party on Mount Olympus – the most exclusive venue in the world, which actually was located on one of Mount Olympus's many peaks.

As he came-to a couple hours later the telescreen was showing an episode of "Switch 'Em" where a billionaire was being interviewed at his immaculate rural Georgia estate, preparing to switch places with a retail worker from the west coast.

"I think it will be tough to be essentially cooped up in the same storefront for 30 hours this week, but I know I can handle it. It will be an interesting experience – certainly something new to be going to work at a solid building everyday instead of just telecommuting online."

Trix rolled his eyes as he flicked off the TV "Pff, asshole."

He put his jacket on and walked downstairs to find something to eat. He briefly considered going to the church for dinner, then decided it wasn't worth hearing the religious volunteers give their "God saves" spiel.

Instead he decided to head 15 blocks to the main food market, where he could fill up on samples from all the vendors; maybe even get a free beer if he saw someone he knew. "*I bet they don't have beers at the church*," he thought as he stepped onto the sidewalk, and lit a cigarette. He looked down and realized he only had two left. Tomorrow he would have to find enough money for another pack somehow. He didn't bother picking up the dirty bank coin worth a half dollar that he noticed at his feet.

"Trix, how are you doing?" Officer Themis was just walking by, and his tone suggested he actually cared how Trix was doing.

"Just planning my next hustle," Trix replied dryly.

"Just don't hustle me." Themis joked. "Hey you know Corner Cop Security still has a few grants available for people who want to get clean. You should see some of these rehab centers, it's like a vacation. There's – "

"Am I being detained?" Trix interrupted. Officer Themis let out a confused laugh, thinking Trix was joking.

"What, no?" Themis replied with a smile.

"Have a good day officer," Trix said emotionless without smiling, and walked away towards the vendor district.

Officer Themis watched him walk away, wishing there was something he could do to help. As Trix turned the corner Themis sighed, shook his head, and continued the beat. Themis was offended and a bit hurt that Trix had asked if he was being detained. That was usually something people without security asked overzealous cops as a way to disengage.

Asking "am I being detained" forced an officer to admit he suspected you of nothing and allow you on your way, or move ahead with procedures. But if the procedures were trumped up, then the officer could lose his job, or be prosecuted if he initiated force. Security agencies were not about to hire or retain officers whose unjust actions they had to spend money defending.

And even if someone didn't have security insurance, he could buy some after a crime was committed against him. Although this was more expensive, if the perpetrator was caught and determined guilty, he was generally made to cover the costs to the victim.

Trix had obviously meant the phrase as an insult after Officer Themis mentioned the rehab grants his security company offered as charity. It bothered Themis since he had come into contact with Trix before over some petty crime and wanted to help him, seeing the best in Trix, but he knew not to be too sensitive.

Officer Themis was the head investigator for violent crime for Corner Cop Security. Since violent crimes only occurred on CCS's customers once every few weeks, the rest of his time was spent patrolling customers' property, like the street he was walking along. His shift ended as the sun started to set, so Themis grabbed a level 2 pod and headed home.

Themis was a friendly outgoing man in his mid thirties, happily married to a teacher; they had two young kids, a boy and a girl. Officer Themis was a good looking man with prominent cheekbones and a strong jawline. He had dark hair, but was relatively pale for modern times. Themis was in shape with a muscular build, he worked out regularly, and practiced regularly with his 9mm – though he had never used it on the job. He was not especially tall, but people seemed to think of him as taller than he actually was.

His darker, equally stunning wife was making dinner when Themis walked in. "Hi James, how was work? Oh before I forget, we got our security contract today, I left it up on the screen for you to look at and sign."

Officer – James – Themis kissed his wife hello, "Anything different this year?"

"Just that Atlas Protection is taking care of more in the gaps between CCS's coverage. They'll be carrying out some patrols, nothing that really affects us."

"Somebody is doing things right, I feel like everyone's flocking to AP these days."

"Well they have a great product, I would feel better about traveling further north now, not that I would've worried much before, but you never know! Oh, can you pick up the kids tomorrow from school? I need to stay there late, I'm tutoring after school now on Tuesdays."

Themis's wife was a teacher at Three Rivers Elementary School. It was one of many schools in the area, and was a branch of Three Rivers Education Group which operated an elementary school, a high school, a trade school, and a daycare/after school care.

"That's fine. Are you still tutoring on Thursdays?"

"Yeah, but it's a different group of kids. The Charity Club raised money last semester to hire tutors for some of the kids who get their tuition through grants. Most of them are doing fine, but I'd say about a quarter just don't seem to be able to keep up with the rest of the kids at school. We noticed about 12 of them falling behind, and of course their scholarships are at risk if they don't maintain their grades. Good kids though, just their parents don't have the skills to teach them outside of school what most of the suburban kids get. Some are only second generation in the New England Economy."

"That's interesting," James said, thinking, "Do you have any first generation students?"

"Yea I actually have one this year who came with her parents three years ago from far east Asia, where the New England Economy hasn't spread yet, but she is a great student. She just gets confused with cultural things; certain lessons, the language, the date. Where she is from they didn't keep the old calendar after the collapse. So their year is, I think... 53? 54 maybe. Based on some 'King's' birth," she made quotation marks with her fingers as she said the word king.

"Wow. So you notice more of the kids who grew up in New England, but had parents who came into NEE late that have more trouble?" asked James.

"Well not all of them, but a lot yes, I think because their parents aren't fully integrated, so they aren't getting all the same home life as third or fourth generation students. Well not that their home life is bad... just they don't have the same roots in the culture. We're actually already starting to see fifth generation kids in the younger age groups. One boy, he's only six, his great great grandfather was born inside the walls of the Worcester Food Corp in 2024. And his great great grandfather's parents had been admitted because *the father's* dad knew a lot about electrics, plumbing, and keeping things running, even though he was a janitor before the collapse. It's really interesting to hear some of the stories, I love teaching the history of New England. We're so close to it, that everyone has some connection to the development."

"That's for sure," James agreed, then smirked slyly, "But it's not every day you meet a family that's 100% descendants of the Blackstone Valley settlement founders," and he puffed out his chest and bobbed his head from side to side with his eyebrows raised, sarcastically putting on an air of superiority. His wife just laughed, rolled her eyes, and shook her head as she finished setting the table, and turned to check on dinner.

THREE

It was Thursday at 13:00 in Barry's office.

"Mr. Barry. I came here to get answers for the questions that you left blank on the BER survey twice. Why have you not made available all company and personal earnings and holdings for fiscal years 2113 and 2114?"

"Did I offer you coffee?" asked Barry, pretending to be distracted by his hospitality, faking a polite smile, and acting a little too innocent.

"Twice, as well as tea, and water, and I am fine thank you. Do you intend to answer my questions?"

"You're so serious!" laughed Barry, forced and fake, "I am just trying to be cordial, smooth things over since you seem upset with me." His lips smiled while his eyes frowned. Barry avoided eye contact of more than a second or two, giving him the appearance of an awkward teen.

"I'm upset because my report is still incomplete, and Business Ethics Review prefers to have their articles submitted a full month before publication. It is now barely three weeks until the release date, and you seem to be taking very lightly the good possibility that your agency will be downgraded by BER."

Barry paused, still displaying his fake smile. His demeanor resembled the Grinch caught off guard by Cindy Lou Who asking why he was stealing her Christmas tree. So he thought up a lie, and he thought it up quick.

"I simply needed more time to collect my records, you see? I have my accounting department putting together a report, and I didn't want to miss anything on the form, otherwise it may look like I had intentionally mislead you, which would never be my intention! And as for my personal holdings, I'm not sure I am comfortable sharing that type of information with the world at large."

"It's customary for men in your position to be an open book, so to speak. After all, a lot of people rely on your company for justice, and they deserve to know there are no outside influences contributing to the decisions and policies of Barry Arbitration."

Another pause. "To be honest Ms. Metis" (Molly almost rolled her eyes at the thought of Barry being honest, but caught herself and continued her powerful stare) "I was a bit self-conscious about some of my investments – er – not performing as well as I'd hoped. They have nothing to do with BA," he added quickly, "but could still give a negative impression to customers."

"I think customers deserve to know if the man running their arbitration agency is mishandling his own funds."

Barry finally dropped the fake smile and replaced it with an annoyed appearance, when he was actually more worried than annoyed. "Well I would hardly say I mishandled my money. Some bets just don't pay off as well – "

"There was a comments section in the survey you failed to complete. A simple explanation of why you made the investments and why their value has dropped would have quelled major fears of incompetence without raising suspicions that go along with leaving that section blank."

"You're right Ms. Metis," his fake smile and teenage demeanor was back. "I'll have my accounting department send you a full report."

"We need it from the bank." Molly would not yield.

Barry briefly considered offering Molly another beverage but decided this would just lead to more tension. This time the pause was too long and Molly further lowered her head and raised her eyebrows as if looking over spectacles that did not exist.

"So if you could call them now, and have that report sent to me..." Molly slowly articulated, annoyed, as if explaining something obvious to a student who could not follow simple directions.

"Yes – yes of course." Barry pressed a button on his receiver and was put through to the Bank of New England, the bank Barry Arbitration used for all their accounting and payroll.

BONE was one of many banks that stabilized currencies by buying up various currencies issued by stores and retailers, smaller banks, corporations, and stocks. BONE would then issue their own currency, the purchasing power of which stayed quite constant. BONE was the biggest bank in the northeast and therefore the most popular currency of most New England inhabitants, though a number of currencies were accepted virtually everywhere, and converted based on daily values of the companies, much like stock prices. For this reason some currencies' purchasing power changed daily, which is why stabilizing bank currencies were useful for people to save up without great risk. Company currencies were backed by the value of the company, and their assets, while bank currencies were backed by their holdings of various company currencies, spreading the risk. Company currencies were therefore generally less stable than bank currencies, and would come and go more often.

"I'd like you to send Molly Metis full reports from Fiscal Years 2113 and 2114 for Barry Arbitration."

"And your personal report," Molly added sternly, with an expression of exasperated disbelief.

"Right, and send along my personal report as well," Barry added, trying to keep his tone upbeat. "And there you have it," Barry added as he pushed the disconnect button, flashing the most plastic smile yet.

"And the only other thing I need is your complete insurance report, and expenditure claims from your agencies."

His smile did not return, fake or otherwise. Without acknowledgment Barry buzzed his secretary, "Send Ms. Metis my expenditure claims and insurance reports."

There was a slight pause from the secretary that Molly pretended not to notice, while making a very particular mental note about it.

"Yes sir."

"Thank you very much for your cooperation Mr. Barry, you can find the report on BER's website with the release date of Monday October 14th. We should have your rating by the 8th if you wish to inquire in advance of the release. Have a great day." And with that Molly closed her tablet, and quickly exited the office without another look at Barry.

Mr. Barry waited a moment after the door closed, and took the scotch bottle out of his desk drawer. Before he poured himself a glass, he looked out the window to see Molly descending the stairs to the sidewalk. He briskly walked to his office door and opened it enough to poke his head through. Checking to see that the reception room was empty besides his secretary, he asked, back to his usual curt and snippy tone.

"For God's sake tell me you sent her the redacted version."

"Does a bear crap in the woods?" his secretary snapped without looking up.

Mr. Barry felt a twang of rage in himself before it was quieted by the comfort of having a competent and complicit, though somewhat entitled, secretary. He was grateful that she knew to send along the version of the report where certain items purchased and covered were redacted. This alone would not be cause for alarm among customers and investors, as it was fairly typical for a man in his position to block out some details about purchases, acquisitions, and insurance coverage. Still, Barry knew he was pushing his luck, and was worried that his company's revenue would nose dive if it was downgraded once again.

He silently ducked his head back into his office and gently shut the door. Slowly he walked to his desk and poured himself a tall glass of scotch.

That night Mr. Barry and Mr. Drake met for dinner. Drake had suggested Hillside, but Barry insisted on a less popular restaurant where he wouldn't run into as many familiar faces. Of course formal attire was required, so Mr. Drake and Mr. Barry were dressed similarly to their work attire, but classier.

Formal clothes were reminiscent of just before the collapse, but with some notable differences. Blazers and suit jackets didn't have any buttons, and were hardly ever made to close, but when they were, it was with poly-melding-elastomer. This synthetic rubber-like material was made to bond and fuse together to form a seal, but could easily be touch activated to release to its old form.

Poly-melding-elastomer replaced zippers and other fasteners, and its use extended beyond clothing. Many high-end windows and doors would seal with poly-melding-elastomer for more efficient insulation. Reusable food containers made of poly-melding-elastomer had become quite popular lately, forming to the food and sealing without air pockets, or molding to any shape needed to fit in the refrigerator or storage and remain firm. But the material could always return perfectly to its initial state.

Whole garments were made of poly-melding-elastomer as well. For sports and physical activity, the clothing would regulate how much air was allowed through the garment based on body temperature. A shirt would increase ventilation during hot weather, and seal shut if it got too cold. Poly-melding-elastomer was a favorite for chiseled men and well endowed women, who's clothing would form fit and seal to accentuate their features. And they never had to buy a new size, as the material would expand or contract naturally, as needed, even as they breathed. poly-melding-elastomer gloves and belts always fit perfectly. There were even anti-rape poly-melding-elastomer undergarments coded to unseal only under specific circumstances. It would be hard to find a home without something made from the new high tech material.

But any poly-melding-elastomer that Drake and Barry wore was well hidden, so that they would not appear tacky. The collars of their shirts were much thinner than pre-collapse collars, or sometimes only an outline with a different material, flush with the rest of the jacket. Dress shirts were also closed with poly-melding-elastomer so that there were no buttons, and only smooth cloth could be seen down the front of the formal shirt. The neck was wider, collar less prominent, and no one wore ties anymore. Instead a "badge" would be worn on the center of the chest, about three quarters of the way up the dress shirt.

Badges attached magnetically or with poly-melding-elastomer, depending on the design of the badge and shirt. Some were small like an old tie clip, but others, especially for formal occasions could be quite large. Most companies had their own insignia, in various sizes and styles, which employees would wear for work; however for personal wear, badges were quite varied.

Drake wore a pure silver badge – except for the poly-melding-elastomer back that attached to a strip of the material on the front of the shirt – which bore his family crest. The coat of arms was engraved with a dragon holding a sword in one hand, and scale in the other. The seal was created by Drake's grandfather when he adopted the family name Drake in the late 2030's after Food Corp operations expanded beyond its walls. Drake's grandfather had been ashamed of how his family raised him before the collapse, and disgusted with the things they did to survive after the collapse. For a range of reasons it was common for people to take a new last name after the collapse, with a strong influence of history and mythology.

Barry wore a badge the size of a large coin that had a black sapphire set in glazed Brazilian rosewood. Barry was a pre-collapse family name, his grandfather was on the board of directors for Food Corp and never suffered much upset during the collapse and New England Renaissance.

"All I need is for the wrong person to see us together and there will be more wild accusations about collusion." Barry hissed.

"For God's sake Barry we aren't the first arbiter and security CEO to ever eat dinner together." Drake said looking up from his touch screen menu as Barry sat down, glancing around to make sure no one he knew was in the dimly lit basement bistro.

"Well with the way BER is up my ass it wouldn't take much right now, with their...erroneous and... flippant..." Barry stumbled as he searched for words to express his anger in an intelligent sounding way.

Drake calmly set his menu down, and offered an amused smile; though a smile on Drake's face was hardly detectable. Slight dimples could be made out however, and his bulldog cheeks were raised, ever so minimally.

"Well I wouldn't exactly call it erroneous... You *did* take the bribe after all."

"And why shouldn't I? I work hard everyday, aren't I entitled to a bonus? Don't I deserve to offer my services outside of the typically expected products arbitration can deliver?" Barry shot back quickly and defensively as 3 slow chuckles made Drake's head bob. "And you'll drop me as soon as the report comes out, don't try to claim otherwise."

"Well," Drake shrugged, "If you get downgraded I might have no other option. Believe me Barry, I am not too keen on the idea of spending more money for less favorable arbitration outcomes."

"This whole thing is just a big mess I don't want to have to deal with! And now my retirement is in jeopardy! I can't even sell the business if I get downgraded, I'll get peanuts, I'll be destitute!"

"You could always move into an adap." Drake joked dryly.

Barry's stare burned of indignation as he spoke a bit too loudly, "Could you take this a bit more seriously Drake! Aren't we friends? I could use some support!"

"Of course, of course," Drake glanced quickly around and made a calming motion with his hand, telling Barry to take it down a notch.

Barry lowered his voice, leaned in, and continued venting. "There's too much competition these days. Remember 20, 30 years ago how easy it was? We were still the first kids on the block, and people needed us! We were running the world and should have done something to keep it that way while we had the chance. Now we're just slowly bleeding to death while these go-getters pull the carpet right out from under us!"

"Speak for yourself, bleeding to death," Drake drawled without glancing up from his menu.

"Ha! I know how your business is doing Drake, you're just as doomed as I am," Barry picked up his glass of wine and gestured to it before taking a sip, "We should enjoy *this* while it lasts. Pretty soon we'll be swigging little more than spiked grape juice."

Drake was annoyed, but his annoyed expression looked pretty much like his normal expression, and only slightly drearier than his "joyful" expression.

"Well to be honest, I had been thinking about the same thing. Running a business these days isn't like it was when my grandfather started NESA. No one knew what was going on back then, and people like him were able to corner the market. Took a long time for anyone to catch up."

"Yes," replied Barry darkly, happy to have Drake agreeing with him. "And before that, in the days of government, people in our positions never had to give up what we had earned. Men like us were set for life, pensions, tenure, the treasury of a whole continent at our disposal. But today, despite the *years* of service, we can still be pushed out and left to die in the cold like a stray dog!" Barry finished dramatically, biting into a fresh caught crab cake brought over by a silent waiter. Still chewing Barry continued, "Of course, some places still have governments. Things would be different if we were born in Korea or even Texas."

"Yea but Korea's a shit-hole, and in Texas judges and security chiefs couldn't pay for this dinner with a month's salary. Even ruling those countries wouldn't put us where we are now."

"But how long can we stay where we are now?! I *thought* that million I put into Transcend Space Travel would pay off, but they've had setback after setback. They said they would be able to travel to Mars by now in under a week." He was talking with his hands, one still holding half a crab cake, and a full mouth, crumbs dropping onto the table. "I can't keep my company afloat with today's competition! I've been racking my brain and I can't think of what to do! If only that bitch Molly would – " He stopped himself.

"Would what?" Drake chuckled.

"Die!" Barry blurted out loudly, laughing; it became apparent to Drake that Barry must have been drinking since noon.

A slightly more detectable smile crossed Drake's face. But he let a good time pass before speaking, just in case Barry had attracted any attention.

"We do seem to be in a unique position to help each other out. You know there is one particular firm that has been sucking up my customers."

"Atlas no doubt", Barry chimed in obliviously, helping himself to another crab cake.

A shudder of fury boiled up inside Drake, and he closed his eyes for a moment to quiet it before speaking.

"Yes. Atlas. But I see an opportunity for us both to benefit, Barry." Drake said his name because he wasn't sure Barry was paying attention. Here Drake was, trying to propose a solution, and Barry seemed to care more about hors d'oeuvres and wine.

"What's that?" replied Barry, mouth full, his moments-earlier bad mood seemed to have been quelled by good food and good wine.

"Well..." Drake briefly considered dropping the subject, but continued. "Atlas is prosecuting that murderer, Ted, from the Cape. The real sick one with the trust fund. It's an open and shut case. He obviously did it. But Atlas just so happens to own some stock in Ted's daddy's brewing and distilling company, Illicit Liquors."

"So how's that going to help us?" Barry was beckoning to the waiter to bring more wine, so Drake, annoyed, waited for the waiter to leave the area before continuing.

"So if it turned out the case wasn't so open and shut, it may look like Atlas *wanted* little Teddy to be prosecuted, to save the business from crumbling when he takes it over."

"Well that doesn't really make much sense, unless Atlas owned some big percentage of the company. How much stock does he have?"

"Practically nothing, but it doesn't need to make sense, it just needs to be widely believed. The story is that Atlas owns a piece of the distilling company, and wants to make sure it succeeds at all costs. We can get the story out, and if we repeat it enough times, people will believe it. You should know that from all the history books you read."

Barry chuckled, "Yes, but in the history books, everybody and their brother didn't own a news website. They just had to get a handful of people to agree, and the world would believe whatever they passed down to their minions."

"We can handle the media," said Drake who owned a controlling stake in a popular area news site, News of New England, and had some connections to others with Internet companies. He figured he'd just pay off the right people, and reimburse himself later by extorting money from Ted's family for the favorable outcome.

Barry put down the knife he was using to butter his roll, finally catching on to Drake's plan. His stressed out demeanor returned as he realized this meal was meant for more than fraternizing.

"But how could I do anything about that. BA isn't even involved in the case."

"No, but if a conflict of interest arose for the arbiters on the case, it would be moved, and if I give Teddy's father a nudge and a wink, I think we could get Barry Arbitration involved in the case."

"And then I commit career suicide by putting my neck on the chopping block when its found out that my ruling was false!" Barry was not convinced. "I could be confined to an adap for that, and what do I get in return? Nothing." Barry was shaking his head no.

"Nothing?" Drake gave a small snort and sigh, "You get to be rid of a certain reporter, and have certain files of hers go missing as well. In the shock and confusion, the report from Business Ethics Review never comes out, and no one pays attention to Barry Arbitration's rating."

"Oh," Barry was taken aback, surprised that the plan had escalated so quickly. "I see. But that still doesn't protect me from it coming to light that I lied about the evidence in the murder case. I'd just be digging my hole deeper, and kicking the can down the road."

"Only if we stop there" Drake retorted.

"Where else is there to go? I undermine your main competitor's credibility, saving your business. You bury a negative report, saving my business... until it is found out that I blatantly lied, at which point I become a confine until I die."

"Well that's where the rest of the plan comes in. Molly's murder won't be just any murder. It will be a drug cartel murder of an innocent, beautiful young women." Drake hadn't planned on discussing this in such detail, but he was too excited, and was planning out loud as much to convince himself as Barry.

Drake had been dreaming this plan up for a while, but now added the details from recently emerging circumstances. "Only the 9th murder this year in all of New England, quickly followed by the 10th, 11th, and 12th – the victims strategically chosen to both elicit fear that no one is safe, even the rich, and take out the people who would most stand in our way. We make it brutal, we frame outside cartels, and we scare people into demanding a border. A border which we control."

"And when other agencies protest the border," Barry said, staring somewhere behind Drake, thinking as he spoke and becoming visibly excited, "BA shows 'evidence' that they are working for the drug cartels, meaning the only ones that can be trusted are ourselves and our partners!"

"Then NESA graciously provides patrols free of charge to anyone within the border," Drake continued, "cutting out the business of whatever security companies are left. We take enough of whatever is coming into our territory on roads and magnet tubes that we control – a sort of tariff – in order to pay for these free patrols, and once NESA and its affiliates are all that's left, impose a tax on the population."

"We trump up charges against other arbiters, or absorb them – pick the right ones to form branches of government with the right positions as bargaining chips," Barry was now smiling with wide eyes, taken away by the possibilities of Drake's plan for power, like a child planning his first trip to Disney World: "I become the Minister of Arbitration, you the Minister of Security, and from there on out it's easy street! Just like pre-collapse!"

Drake's smile was more detectable than usual, "Bingo!" he drawled as he raised his eyebrows and took a sip of his wine.

The better part of a minute passed in silence as the two considered the plan.

"But..." Barry was still thinking, and his smile turned into a sideways frown, skeptical that the plan could fall into place, "It would be *such* a risk."

"All great men once took a great risk," argued Drake calmly. "But we have this opportunity once, before our businesses decline or come crumbling down. It's now or never."

"How would we put it all into motion though, without it getting away from us?"

"Just leave that to me, I know who to talk to, I know who I can trust. I've already done some probing and testing, so to speak."

Barry wasn't convinced, and he took a deep breath and let it out slowly. "I need to be sure. I can't just throw caution to the wind with nothing but your assurance."

The two fell silent as their food arrived. The juiciest pink-in-the-middle fillet mignon – rarer these days as people were used to much less meat in their diets, and cattle raising never resumed on the same scale after the collapse. On the side were mashed potatoes with garlic and real butter, grilled asparagus, assorted raw leafy greens topped with goat cheese and a raspberry vinaigrette, lamb-broth gravy with mushrooms and onions, lobster tail with a cream sauce topped by caviar, and olive oil painted dinner rolls with herbs that looked like an artist had prepared them for a museum.

"Listen," Drake began as he lowered his voice and cut into his steak, placing a bloody, dripping morsel into his mouth, and chewing, "We can handle the media. We have more to offer with this plan than money, we can now offer power, straight up, unadulterated force, used for whatever they desire. So we set up Ministries, and sell the positions to those with the most power. I happen to have the right connections in the news world so that we can control the very thing which will advance us to the next level; it will be state propaganda... like the Soviet days." Drake added, knowing Barry's obsession with history, particularly dictatorships.

"I'm reading about Joseph Stalin now!" Barry exclaimed, excited to add value to their relationship.

Drake acted as if he hadn't heard Barry, and he was so wrapped up in his plan that he indeed might not have heard. "We might need some strategic Internet blackouts, but we can take care of that with a couple of false flag killings, and then some raiding of the right businesses. But the key is that the things going wrong must look like it is society disintegrating around the people. And when my men arrive on the scene everything is righted, and NESA is the hero. BA will apply the law as it currently stands in the most common contracts, but you will be the only arbitration agency left, so there will be no one to check up on the rulings, the evidence, and the convictions. We purge the detractors by charging them with crimes connected to the cartels, or crimes destabilizing the region." Drake wasn't even talking to Barry anymore, and Barry sensed this, feeling left out for a moment.

"And we'll call Barry Arbitration New England Arbitration for cohesion!" Barry slammed his fist on the table a bit harder than intended, and his half full glass of wine spilled onto the white tablecloth, creating a deep red stain like blood, as Barry let slip an expletive.

Drake was brought back to reality and looked at Barry with a note of agitation and slight disappointment in his face as the waiter rushed over to clean up the mess, "Yes, that *is* a good idea", and he did in fact like the idea of renaming the agencies to match the new state.

Barry turned a little red in the cheeks at his mishap, and the two ate in silence for a minute or two. Barry was coming back to his senses, and again starting to worry about the potential for the plan to go awry.

"But can you imagine if we got caught, Drake, how terrible the remainder of our lives would be, like dogs in a kennel," Barry was almost whining.

"As opposed to your life now? As a house-trained dog who's got to wag his tail and lick the hand of his owners that we call customers? A man leashed by the market, who barks on command, and who is about to be put down by some bitch vet because you pissed on the wrong fire hydrant?"

Drake is quite the orator, Barry thought. Barry was comforted by his friend's conviction, and more convinced as Drake's confidence about their plan shined through his normally sullen face. In reality Drake had only convinced himself that the plan would work while explaining it at dinner. And Drake was comforted by his minion's support.

The truth was that Drake too thought of Barry as a dog, but knew that a dog could be man's best friend. Loyalty from Barry was not in question, and Drake knew that all Barry needed were a few pats on the head, and Barry would growl and flash his teeth at anyone who his master deemed an enemy.

Barry was thinking hard, and couldn't decide what he wanted. The plan did sound great to him – well definitely the end result. And pleasing Drake was another huge plus; and with a man like Drake at the wheel it did seem more likely to Barry that they would see success.

But the risk! This was an all-in moment, and Barry was not the type to make tough decisions. As much as he hated being chained to the market, he had always tended to rely on popular demand of the customers to guide his actions; the reason he was successful in the first place. But here he was, one man who had to decide whether to take the risk with such an immense potential reward, but with such dire possible consequences.

Barry was used to betting with his money, but he had never bet with his freedom before. But then true power, in the old sense, had never been on the table. He felt like this was the reward that his whole life was building up to, and to give up on power would leave him only money – which was already at risk because of the pending BER report.

Barry thought that even if he did manage to hold onto his business, and maintain profits, what more could he look forward to in life? The very probable possibility of diminishing profits and less spending money only added to the desire to take this bet, and risk it all. Barry was shaking his head, gazing up in thought, biting and pursing his lips in quick and random succession. As his mind swayed from yes to no and back his body could practically be seen mimicking the thought process, like a drunk man trying to catch his balance after standing up too quickly.

"If there was some sort of insurance policy..." Barry pleaded, unable to commit, though wanting so badly to see the plan fulfilled. He was avoiding direct eye contact with Drake.

Drake was staring squarely at Barry. "How hard do you think it is to flee the area, go somewhere that no one will recognize you?"

"Pff," Barry let out a humorless laugh, "any agency in this hemisphere would recognize us through facial recognition eventually, and collect the probably gigantic bounty."

"There are places to go," drawled Drake as if this was obvious. He knew Barry was on the tipping point. "And we are talking worst case scenario."

Barry thought worst case scenario. *Worst case scenario I take off on my yacht and sail the world*. He thought that might not be so bad. Of course that still had its risks if he planned to go ashore at port, but then again he could choose his ports wisely, and perhaps hire people to buy the supplies he needed. Maybe there would be tropical islands without cameras. He would need to have supplies ready to change the appearance of his yacht enough so that it would not be recognized were he to become an outlaw. The idea was romanticized in Barry's head, and he briefly imagined himself as a pirate, before becoming embarrassed at himself for having such a childish thought. But still, the rest sounded plausible. Plausible as a worst case scenario, if the ultimate plan, with the ultimate reward, failed.

"We'll have to do this so that we will get some warning if things sour," Barry was speaking seriously and skeptically. "I'll be on my yacht when it all happens, and I'll want to be in contact with you throughout the entire ordeal. The first one you call as the pieces fall into place. Just don't hang me out to dry."

Drake had convinced him. Drake's face was the brightest Barry had ever seen it, and he swore he could see a full fledged grin for a split second. "I knew you would come to your senses," finished Drake triumphantly as he held up his glass of wine for a toast. "To government."

Barry smiled. He was entering into the most important contract of his life, what it had all led up to, with the best possible partner. He was starting to once again relax.

"To government!" he toasted. *Clink*.

Four

Molly was going over Barry Arbitration's numbers at the office. She was only required to come into the office twice a week, but she was the type that didn't mind the change in scenery from working at home. At the offices of Business Ethics Review there were plenty of workstations of various styles, and each employee had their own small closet to store work items in, to be retrieved and brought to the table, cubicle, or comfortable chair of their choosing. She had one hand in her hair, her elbow resting on the table. The other hand flicked the screen of her extra large tablet, the type ideal for work. It had on one side a 20cm screen, but could also fold out to reveal two 20cm screens which could combine to become flush and form one large screen, or be set at a 45 degree angle with one acting as a keyboard, and the other as the screen to form a laptop.

Molly had the screen on large, lying flat on the table. The earbuds she wore used EEG (electroencephalogram) technology to detect the natural electromagnetic signals the brain gives off. This allowed Molly to take notes without having to physically type anything. She could control virtually anything on her tablet by just thinking if she wanted to, but touch could also be used.

Molly could not believe how much was redacted from Barry's personal report. It was not quite enough to make a big deal out of the redactions alone, but enough to arouse suspicion – or more suspicion in this case. She wanted to bring Barry Arbitration's rating down, because she felt that the company deserved it; but she needed to build her case on solid evidence that readers could understand. As a reporter for Business Ethics Review, Molly's job was to build a case against each company she rated, and present that case to readers. Some businesses were squeaky clean, others had their fair share of baggage. But rarely would a company be found to be so corrupt or unethical as to ruin its business; these revelations became less and less frequent as the years went on, and businesses learned that it was more profitable to remain legitimate.

Luckily, the juiciest news these days was considered corruption in business. This kept companies honest, because so many professional journalists, as well as amateurs, were watching. Since everyday people had pocket sized portables or mini-tabs connected via Internet for video calling, messaging on the go, taking pictures, recording video, and browsing, the news was everywhere.

"Hey Molly, check this out," Molly's boss, Otto, said as he approached with his mini-tab in his outstretched hand. He spoke with a Northern European accent, which sounded like a mix of various pre-collapse accents, notably British and Scandinavian.

Molly took her earbuds out, and looked at the screen. She was used to her bubbly boss interrupting to show her a video or to talk. She didn't mind the break.

"Remember this clip?" Otto asked, eyebrows raised.

It was a shaky video of two men sitting at a table in a fast food joint, taken from the next booth over. They were speaking in hushed whispers conspicuously.

"Yeah," Molly replied thinking back, "This was the owner of the packaging facility bribing the reporter to keep quiet, right?"

"Yes and with facial recognition they were both identified and everyone learned of the *heaps* of rat shit in one of the facilities that the reporter had uncovered on a surprise visit." Otto spoke quickly with much expression. He drew in a large breath and continued, "Well it was 6 days ago that the kid who shot the clip sold it to us, and today the entire packing company has closed, for good. Done! I think that's a new record for BER!" Otto excitedly finished with a geeky smile and two thumbs up.

"Wow!" Molly was impressed, "Were all the factories just as bad?"

Otto launched into a new round of eager explanation, "No! It was just the one that had anything wrong with it, but once we broke the story we got *millions* of hits in the first several hours. It went viral. And when the *same* facility was checked again the situation had already been righted, but by that point the reporter had already sold us the *original* footage to try to save face."

"And no one even got sick? If the owner had just come clean and apologized he probably could have saved his business," Molly exclaimed with a dry laugh, shaking her head in disapproval.

Otto nodded with an almost sympathetic closed mouth smile, and then he was onto the next subject. "So how's the Barry Arbitration rating going?"

"Eh, its fine," Molly sat back and gave a light sigh.

"Ah, well I think this is going to shape up to be another one of the classic Molly Metis-" Otto made a smashing motion and sound effects, "-destroyers!"

"Oh please," Molly laughed, "I haven't ruined *that* many businesses. And they were all bad!"

"Still, my favorite was when you audited and brought down the bankers skimming their currency," Otto acted like he had just tasted something exquisite, touching his fingers to his lips with a kissing sound. "Perfect! When I saw the bank close and sell off its assets, I marched right up to the Head Editor for Business Ethics Review, I shoved my portable in his face and I said, hire this woman! And not only did each bank board member get *ten years* in confinement, but they had to forfeit their assets and serve the sentence in adaps!" Otto burst out laughing. "I love it!"

Special advertisers' apartments were built by security firms to house certain guilty criminals, who were confined to the adap. They would be allowed to socialize with other confines (pronounced with the emphasis on the first syllable) at designated times. Some of the funds from the forfeiture would be used to give confines a weekly allowance which they could only spend on specific items, ordered through controlled closed network vacuum shipping tubes. Of course all the food, hygiene, and the few other items sold were advertised on the walls, and this helped fund the confinement adaps as well.

While this was a typical setup for the punishment of a crime, it was certainly not the only one. When the guilty party did not lose his assets in arbitration, he was often placed under house arrest in his own home and fitted with a tracker, or sometimes limited house arrest with some ability to travel still permitted. It all depended on the seriousness of the crime, and the sentence negotiated during arbitration. There were a handful of serious criminals in New England actually still held in an old style prison at the offices of various security companies, but this was rare, and only applied for crimes like premeditated murder and rape. Of course the rare instances of rape and murder were made even more rare since a good percentage of *attempted* rape and murder ended in the death of the attacker.

"They're the minority though," Molly humbly downplayed her skills. "Most of my cases play out in the court of public opinion."

"Just as useful! Sometimes hitting them right in the bank account is the most appropriate punishment anyway!" Otto said as he made a slow punching motion. "Anyway keep up the good work, you are invaluable to me and to this company, and I shudder to think what businesses the good people of New England would patronize without your journalism to guide them!"

And with that, Otto was off leaving Molly smiling and shaking her head modestly. *It feels good to be appreciated.*

Molly had been courted by a few different arbitration agencies, some offering her a decent raise compared to her current journalist salary, but she loved reporting, and did fine financially. If she went into arbitration, Molly thought she would want to start her own firm. She had been laying quite the foundation for a solid career in the field with her high-quality-reports over the past decade.

Molly was becoming something of an expert on the interactions of people and groups. The non-aggression principle was the foundation for modern common law – no victim, no crime – but there were always disputes on what constituted aggression, and what the victim could do to respond. She studied these cases, analyzing arbitration outcomes and retribution, in order to better scrutinize arbitration agencies and security companies.

For instance, an "equal and opposite reaction" was considered appropriate for a violation of a person's rights. This meant that if someone trespassed on your property without knowing it, the appropriate response was to escort them off, and shooting them would not be considered an "equal" reaction to the violation (unless of course they had exhibited violent behavior towards the property owner).

Molly learned over time that it was a fine line for arbiters to walk, keeping their customers happy, but also making sure that outsiders were treated fairly. Otherwise the legitimacy of the arbiter would falter, and companies and individuals would stop doing business with them out of fear of unfair treatment themselves, or the desire to not be party to aggression. Vigilant patrons and the public policed arbitration agencies which had on some occasions gone under after a single misstep.

Even less important businesses were not immune to rapid boycott, when it became an overnight faux pas to patronize them. This sometimes happened if it got out that an employee, or a customer had been treated poorly, or if an adap expelled a zero-profit-generating-tenant. The fear of public backlash also contributed to why companies like UtopaCorp would hire pretty much anybody as long as they were willing to follow their rules.

Molly also found it useful and interesting to study groups who did not like the commercial world. Some people preferred to exit it completely, or only use the modern economy for certain high tech medical needs, or the occasional harder-to-come-by product. There were plenty of little neighborhoods and communities around where like-minded people joined together to form their own mini economy. Most of these were agriculture-based, involving many people who enjoyed working outside and with their hands making natural products and living a simpler life. Or sometimes their lives would be just as high tech, but the inhabitants just preferred to consort with their selected group. They would often have their own systems of property ownership and conflict resolution.

Only in extremely rare cases did a security company have to visit these mini societies for a breach of contract on behalf of an outside victim. And like businesses, if the microcosm cared about their public image – which admittedly some of them didn't – they would give the occasional interested reporter a taste of what life was like in their world, and let the public know if they were free to join, they had to know someone, or couldn't get in even if they wanted too.

Over the decades a few sketchy cult-like communities cropped up, but each time a victim would leave and the perpetrators would be brought to justice on the victim's behalf when the word got out, collapsing the settlement. There were groups that performed a charity service of finding victims of crimes who could not, for whatever reason, find protection, or bring the assailant to justice. Also, professional bounty hunters made it so that criminals had nowhere to hide in the shrinking world where you could get practically anywhere on earth within 8 hours from some combination of modern travel – usually magnet pods, but also space planes, and skyships.

But there were plenty of places the mag-pods didn't go, because the people in the area had no interest. Or, in some areas just one pod terminal was required for thousands of residents, for occasional long distance travel.

The midwest of North America was host to several large societies with preordained rules that people had to follow in order to live there. The land would be owned by one person or group, and in order to rent or buy it, the buyer would have to agree to the owner's rules, and this was the basis for "law" in the region. The attraction was bundled services and a sense of community.

In this way it was much like a town, where if people liked the system set up by the property owner, they would move there, and if not, they would move away. When major grievances arose against a town or city (i.e. if crime rates rose, or it was hard to do what you wanted), it was common to see a rival town spring up just miles away, attracting the disenfranchised folks from the other place. Since these towns were run like corporations, attracting townspeople with good rules and convenient services was necessary, and this created constant competition to form better and better towns where people wanted to live.

If a town became a cartel, and forced their will on people in a particular area without their consent, there were plenty of companies for hire that would set them straight, backed by arbiters who would essentially legitimize a company's response to violations of others' rights, by investigating, weighing the evidence, and offering guidelines and backing for an appropriate response.

In other communities rules were looser, and shunning was the most practical form of punishment for non-serious crimes. The Amish carried on, pretty much as they always had, and other groups adopted a more technologically advanced and less repressive version of their societies.

The so-called "social contract" was not forced on people based on geography, but was rather agreed to by people deciding to join a community or not. Since there were many options, anyone could easily choose another microcosm to inhabit without having to move around the world... although moving around the world was *also* pretty easy. And some people just decided to go live alone, or with a small group, take their protection into their own hands, make and grow most of what they needed and otherwise find those to trade with. They weren't bothered by anyone who valued his own life and freedom.

And there it was, the crack in Barry's records. Molly jolted to attention as she saw that Barry had used 5,000 units of a particular currency to pay bills in the last two years, while only officially bringing in 2,000 units. Since the currency was introduced two years ago, it was impossible that he had retained some from earlier years. It *was* however possible, that the money was acquired legitimately from the private sale of assets, or investment income – though the latter was unlikely based on Barry's claim that his hesitation on providing records was due to his investments performing poorly. Molly's next step would be to check into any sales Barry made of homes, vehicles or other large assets over the last two years, which she began immediately, invigorated by her find. It was like solving puzzles to Molly; this was why she loved her job so much.

Trix sat in his adap, watching TV. He was trying to hold off on getting high for a couple more hours so that he wouldn't have to buy more drugs that day, and he could save the few dollars he had scrounged together. He was thinking about getting a decent meal for once. Of course his version of a decent meal was fast food – healthier than pre-collapse fast food, but still the worst option out there. When the wall with video ads popped up with an advertisement for the Sandwich Shack, showing a grilled fish sandwich from all angles, complete with fire potatoes and carbonated ice tea, his mind was made up. He flicked off the TV, and left the adap to stop by the Sandwich Shack.

Some Sandwich Shacks were small buildings, while others were just booths or kiosks with one or more stations, but none of them had full time workers. The busiest and upscale locations had a service technician standing by during peak hours, but most were only visited by company employees for cleaning and maintenance. The ingredients were shipped in through vacuum tubes fed directly into fast food units.

It was only one block for Trix to the nearest street kiosk for the Sandwich Shack; just two wall units right off the sidewalk, with nowhere to sit. Trix simply walked up to the screen on the sidewalk and ordered from the digital menu. Everything was automated, and his meal popped out next to him in the cubby with a clear hatch that unlocked when the order was ready. The hatch lifted, and Trix took his meal on the tray, and transferred it into one of the to-go bags provided.

Fried food had never made an immense resurgence since the New Dark Ages and the aftermath when cooking oil was more scarce, and would instead be used to coat potatoes – or more often dandelion root or Jerusalem artichoke – and bake them causing a similar crispy effect. But grilling had been the most popular cooking method after the collapse, over wood fire usually, except inside Food Corp where they still used mostly electric stoves and ovens. Soda had turned into various carbonated beverages from flavored water, to the more typical sweetened drink, as well as a plethora of sparkling juices and concoctions.

Trix decided to take a short walk to eat his meal in a park paved with white stone, on a bench under some oak and maple trees. There was a fountain in the middle made of marble, with the water pouring out of a man's cupped hands. It was the owner of the adjacent outdoor shopping plaza who had built the park to attract shoppers and allow them to enjoy the scenery while shopping or with their food, and he was vain enough to place his own marble likeness prominently at an entranceway.

Every bite of the fish sandwich tasted so delicious to Trix that he wondered for a second if he was high, before realizing the natural joy he was getting from a simple meal. So he slowed down and made sure to soak in the moment, a rare one that felt good without drugs. It was later afternoon before he got back to his adap, having taken the long way home to enjoy the weather for a nice walk.

He was also trying to prolong his time sober. He had nowhere to go but home, and knew that once he got home he would just get high. It depressed him, only because he had found simple joy in eating his lunch. Even when he arrived back in his apartment, as the advertisements flickered on talking about vacationing in Iceland, he actually scooped some of the trash that was on the floor into the bin, pushed it down with a greasy box, tied it, and threw it down the garbage shoot at the end of the hall. The shoot led to trash pods, transported to waste management facilities through the same main pod system used for travel. He couldn't find any other trash bags though... in fact Trix wondered how he had gotten the last one.

Trix then spent another minute or two making things a bit neater in his adap, although it mostly amounted to moving things from one place to another, perhaps placed in slightly more organized piles. Then he flicked on the TV, grabbed his EZject, plopped down on his mattress, packed up the cartridge, and injected. Trix drifted off imagining himself in a geyser fed natural hot tub and taking a mud bath.

The agents did not wear any identifying insignia. Efforts had been taken to obscure where their pay stemmed from – their pay was kept off the books, as was their job description. The two agents wore suits typical of an investigator, inconspicuous, dark, with mundane silver- colored badges. They also wore sunglasses so no one could tell where they were looking. The sunglasses were screen lensed; the agents had all the best technology and any piece of relevant information literally right in front of their eyes, controlled by thought with EEG detectors. The first time they visited this adap building they followed the GPS on their tiny screens, but this time they remembered where it was.

The two agents could be mistaken for brothers with their glasses on, because they were about the same height, late thirties, average to muscular build, strong-jawed, confident eyes, and a tendency to wear the slightest smirk on their face, as if they were getting the better of everyone they met. Their eyes, apart from the similar tenacity, showed the difference of the two that no one ever saw. The difference that *was* noticed by those who dealt with the two agents was their good cop/bad cop personas, and their hair. "Good cop" was referred to as Agent White who had the lighter hair, blue eyes, and a slightly smaller build, and "bad cop" was Agent Orange, dark haired speckled with gray, brown eyes and square shoulders. They were self branded names that the partners found humorous. They adopted this persona in order to fulfill their jobs, which *usually* bordered on legitimate, but on the wrong side of the line.

They would deliver messages and arrange certain meetings. They would hire particular types of employees for one time jobs, sometimes clean up a mess themselves, or do the dirty work in rough investigations. But officially they had no business with anyone. Those for whom they fulfilled contracts wanted to be able to distance themselves from the agents, if the need arose.

They walked through the wide hallway of the adap with kiosks and shops lining the walls, and took the elevator to the second floor. The advertisements were random, since technology in the agents' glasses jammed the facial recognition which would have tailored the ads. They walked only a few feet down the hall before stopping in front of a door with chipping paint. Agent White knocked.

Trix was sitting up on his mattress slumped with his back against the wall, staring in the general direction of the TV. He was actually focused behind the TV, distracted by the ad on the screen wall in the background which was promoting some brand of toilet paper. There were some strange animated animals soaring through the sky with a rainbow trailing behind them. The EZject was lying on the floor a few inches away from his upward facing palm which was relaxed on the floor, his left arm hanging off the mattress.

At the first knock Trix didn't seem to notice the slight banging on the door, on the second knock he slowly turned to look at the door, as if he would be able to see through it. His mouth drooped slightly open with a little dried white drool on either side of his lips, his eyes half closed, with each blink lasting longer than usual. Trix felt like each time his eyes closed a wave crashed over his apartment, and as they reopened the wave receded back into the ocean, complete with the shwoosh sound of lightly pounding currents, and the feeling of being immersed in cool salty water with fractured light flickering through.

On the third knock Trix finally responded, "Whoisit?" a bit slurred.

"It's Agent White, open up Trix," the agent said calmly.

There was a pause. "I don't have to let you in," Trix slowly responded without moving, in the same emotionless tone.

"Yea, but you probably want to," Agent Orange chimed in, with a smirk infecting his voice.

Silence. The two agents exchanged a glance and waited.

"It's a job offer Trix," Agent White added in a tone of comforting a sick child.

Another twenty seconds passed before the door was opened part way, and Trix's tired face, still expressionless peeked out.

"Can we talk inside?" White said in the same tone.

Trix turned and walked into his apartment, leaving the door open for the Agents to come in. He sat down on his bed as the agents glanced around, again exchanged a quick look, and remained standing facing Trix as he lethargically lit a cigarette.

Agent White stood with his hands clasped, arms relaxed. Agent Orange stood with his arms crossed.

"We have a job offer for you Trix, but it's a little more serious than last time. You're not going to be simply transferring a suitcase." Agent White explained. Trix wasn't looking at them. The agents waited for a response.

"So? What is it?" asked Trix annoyed, finally looking up at the agents with bloodshot eyes.

"Well, first..." Agent Orange took an envelope out of his jacket pocket, "We want you to see what we're offering." He tossed the envelope onto the bed next to Trix.

Trix took another drag on his cigarette, and left it in his mouth as he reached for the envelope without excitement. "Jesus," it was an exclamation though subdued and emotionless. "Do I even *want* to know what the job is?" Trix flicked the envelope back onto the bed where Agent Orange had tossed it. A few of the fifteen notes were visible. They were each 100 unit notes from AtlantiTrade.

AtlantiTrade was a worldwide investment firm that traded stocks, bought up currencies, and issued their own currency. It was so widespread with so many various transactions taking place that it was a difficult currency to track, being preferred by those who didn't want anyone to find out where particular funds came from or went. While the notes were coded to prevent forgeries, the codes were encrypted so that AtlantiTrade didn't know which notes had been issued or redeemed by particular individuals depositing or withdrawing them from banks. One unit of AtlantiTrade was worth about 35 dollars. The agents were offering 1,500 units.

"So what do you think Trix, are you interested?" Agent White asked.

"You haven't told me what I'm supposed to do."

The agents hesitated, and glanced at one another. Agent Orange gave a slight shrug to White. "We need some files to be destroyed, and in the process, we need the owner of those files... deleted as well," Agent White explained, while Agent

Orange smiled and suppressed a chuckle at White's choice of words.

"Pff." Trix shook his head slowly without looking up and took the final drag on his cigarette, putting it out in the ashtray on the windowsill. "I'm not a murderer," he said calmly exhaling the smoke, finally meeting eyes – or sunglasses rather – with the agents.

"Trix," began Agent Orange, as a coach might begin an inspirational speech to an athlete, "sometimes, there are problems that can't be handled in a normal way. Sometimes... the outcome of *not* going above the law would be worse than the suffering caused by letting things play out on their own."

"Forget it, I don't need your money." It was tempting, but Trix wasn't a killer.

The agents exchanged a short glance. "The money was to make this easy Trix, but we aren't asking," Agent White explained calmly. Trix just let out an exasperated sigh and shook his head once, still staring out the window.

A long twenty seconds passed before any of the three moved. Finally Agent Orange reached into his jacket, and pulled out a large antique metallic finished Colt .45, and grabbed Trix by his hair. Before he knew what happened, the barrel of the gun was under Trix's chin and the loud click of Agent Orange cocking the hammer echoed through the bare room. Agent Orange was speaking loudly now, but articulately – not yelling. His jaw was clenched, and he was sternly instructing Trix.

"You are going to go to the address in that envelope, at the time and date it says. You are going to finish off the lady that lives there, and you are going to take her tablet, and take every hard drive in her house, and delete all her files on clouds. You will then throw the hardware into Lake Quinsig, and take a pod out of New England. Then, you're a free man. Are we clear?"

Tears were building up in Trix's eyes and he made a sound that sounded kind of like yes.

"Are we clear?" Agent Orange was almost yelling now as he yanked Trix's hair back harder and pressed the barrel more firmly into Trix's throat.

"Yes!" Trix managed to choke out, his voice cracking, and Agent Orange immediately let him go, and re-holstered his gun without another word. Trix put his head in his arms, shaking, still sitting on the edge of his bed.

Agent Orange walked to the panel controlling the wall advertisements. He took a discrete card out of his pocket, and waved it in front of the receiver: there was money on the card, but nothing to identify the holder. He brushed through a few options screens, and picked a nice green field with flowers slowly swaying in the wind, and a blue sky with wispy clouds floating slowly by to replace the advertisements on the wall.

"Here you go Trix. I bought you an hour."

Agent White squatted down to Trix's level, and put his left hand gently on his shoulder.

"It's just a job Trix, don't let it get to you." He patted Trix's back and with his right hand, reached into his pocket, took out a baggie and put it on the windowsill next to the ash tray.

Agent White stood up, and left the room, followed by Agent Orange. Before closing the door Agent Orange looked toward Trix.

"Don't make us pay you another visit Trix, and I'm sure I don't have to explain how stupid you would have to be to run."

He closed the door, and Trix looked up to make sure the agents were gone. With tears in his droopy eyes he reached for the baggie that Agent White had left on the windowsill, and filled up his EZject. As his body slipped into numbness, an indicator in White's glasses went off. It showed him that the nano-tracker Trix had just injected into his arm with the drugs was active.

Barry was inside his office adjusting his badge – this one with the Barry Arbitration logo – and looking in the mirror to make sure he was well put together. The reporters were waiting in the conference room, where cameras would broadcast Mr. Barry to the news stations, as was customary when high profile rulings came out of an arbitration agency. The reporters all wondered aloud to each other what the conference could possibly be about, since the murder ruling was not due out for another week or so. BA had been coy in getting the news to cover this announcement, promising a big story but giving few details. Molly watched from the receiving room at BER headquarters. Drake tuned in to the News of New England, which he owned a controlling stake in, to watch the conference.

Barry walked into the conference room, and took his place in front of the cameras at the podium. He cleared his throat.

"Thank you for your attention, I've called this conference to announce some troubling news uncovered in the course of arbitration between Atlas Protection and Coastal Security", Barry paused to take a drink of water, and wipe some sweat from his forehead. "In the murder case of Athena Sicily it was found that Atlas Protection manufactured evidence in order to frame Ted Lanta, having no other leads to go on, in the desire to appease the family of the deceased. Evidence suggests Ted was chosen to be framed due to Rand Atlas' investment in the Lanta family's brewing company, Illicit Liquors, with the intention of keeping Ted from taking control of the company."

"When will the evidence be released?" shouted one reporter, in a frantic tone of disbelief.

"Due to the sensitive nature of this investigation, and lack of cooperation from AP, the evidence of AP's wrongdoing will be withheld, pending further review. As of this moment proceedings against Ted Lanta are dropped, and he has been ordered released from Atlas Protection custody. Charges against Atlas Protection are pending. Thank you, all further questions should be submitted through my office." He walked away from the podium, ignoring the concerned uproar and questions being hurled at him by various reporters who were present.

Back at BER headquarters Molly was wide eyed with mouth agape, paralyzed by shock. She knew something was not right about this, and had herself just finished an audit of Atlas Protection's proceedings, which AP had been extremely open about. Suspecting the worst of Barry, she decided to get Kitt's side of the story.

Molly couldn't even get through on her two way screen to Atlas headquarters, waiting on hold for a half hour before deciding to go down to the office in person. The place was a zoo, with employees running from desk to desk, fielding calls on every available screen, and trying desperately to transfer the callers to the correct branch.

"No, no it's not true, we are asking for patience as this is sorted out."

"There's no need to transfer, this is a just a mis-understanding."

"The evidence was not released because there is no evidence. We are working on straightening this out, but it is entirely and categorically false."

These lines and others could be heard throughout the office, like an echo that wouldn't go away. As usual Mr. Atlas' office door was open, and an unusually large volume of employees streamed in and out, with looks on their faces ranging from horror, to exasperation, to steady-handed concern.

Molly managed to squeeze her way in to see Atlas standing at his desk propping himself up with both hands on the surface talking to someone on his video screen.

"That's fine we can pay the extra cost, we just need it done as soon as possible. Thanks."

"Mr. Atlas, I know you must be busy, but I was hoping for a quick conversation."

"Molly, hi," Atlas greeted her, slightly distracted, though he still managed a smile, in a tired sort of way. He walked around his desk and sat on the edge. He was not wearing his typical badge, his hair looked messier than usual, like he had been running his hand through it periodically, and his sleeves were rolled up.

"I think I can spare a few minutes for BER, especially under the circumstances," again the tired smile flashed across his face.

"So I'm assuming it's not true?" Molly blurted out.

"No, its not. We are trying to get that out to all the customers, but as you can see its a mad house in here at the moment. I've commissioned a review from Independent Arbitration, but obviously that will take some time."

"I'll put out a headline about your review... we can't release it early, but I can at least get a press release stating that BER found nothing sinister in its latest review."

"Thank you Molly, that would be great," Mr. Atlas replied somewhat lethargically, managing another smile – a real smile, as exasperated as it may have been.

"And once the report on BA comes out, I know people will change their tune. He's getting downgraded." Molly was sure she would find enough to warrant a downgrade of BA, though she had not yet completed poring through Barry's records. At this point she didn't care how much time she needed to spend and digging she had to do in order to find the inconsistency in the finances. She knew the allegations against AP were false, she had seen all of AP's records herself, and known Kitt Atlas for years.

"If it's not too late by then," Atlas replied, almost to himself, giving a slight shrug, a look of disappointment on his face. "And it's funny, NNE has been repeating over and over that I own stock in the Lanta family's brewing business, like it's a conflict of interest. But if they looked into it, they'd see I own, like, a few thousand dollars' worth of stock. They are making it out like I have some stake in the future of the company. I wouldn't even notice if the company went bankrupt!"

That's strange, Molly thought. *Why would News of New England make such a big deal out of Atlas' tiny amount of stock in the company? Could it just be sensational reporting, or was there something deeper about the connection they were trying to draw?*

"Well, I'm sure you have plenty on your plate right now, let me know if there is anything else I can do to help," Molly concluded as another stream of concerned employees started to enter the office. She turned back before leaving and added, "Don't worry, you'll get through this."

Mr. Atlas smiled and nodded as she left; she had a way of calming his nerves. Kitt admired Molly's strong personality, and laughed at himself as he wondered momentarily what their interactions might have led to if he were 20 years younger. Atlas pushed those thoughts away, refocusing on the many issues at hand. *Publications like BER are what keep situations like these from ruining honest businesses,* he reassured himself.

FIVE

Drake met the CEO of Minutemen Arms, Mr. Patrick, in his office. Mr. Patrick was in his late thirties, tall, not bony, but not muscular. He had dark hair, and dark eyes, with a square-ish chin that made him automatically look confident. In the New England winter he would become a bit pale, and in the summer surprisingly dark. He and Drake had been friends since they started doing business together when Patrick started his security company a decade earlier. Drake had no children, and thought of Patrick as the closest thing to a son.

They were having a normal jovial conversation about a car Mr. Patrick had just bought. Most people didn't own cars these days since there was no real need to with the extensive networks of magnet tunnels. Some people in rural places still found them useful, although anyone with enough money would generally just buy a skyship – a helium filled aircraft that differed from a blimp because it was not lighter than air, had wings like an airplane, and propellers for lift and thrust. Of course, Mr. Patrick also had a couple skyships; his car was just for fun. Cruising down the highways, you would generally only see one or two other cars every minute or so.

Patrick's 300 horsepower coupe, reminiscent of an old corvette, ran on sea weed ethanol, the preferred combustible fuel due to the renewable nature of kelp, and because there was no wasted agriculture space or soil nutrients. Unless you wanted a muscle car, like Patrick, people would just get an electric one, since helium cooled nuclear power was plentiful, and broadcast wirelessly through Tesla inspired coils. Helium became a viable alternative method of cooling nuclear reactors once cheaper methods of helium production were streamlined a decade earlier; and since helium cannot become radioactive, it was safer than using water to cool the reactors.

Wave power and windmills were still plentiful in coastal areas however, accounting for 60% of power in New England north of Boston. And hydroelectric plants on rivers made up close to 10% of New England's overall power needs. Combustible fuels were only rarely used for power, generally to drive backup generators, or to power building and settlements that were remote and disconnected. But power wires were almost nowhere to be seen. Some underground cables still transmitted electricity to the Tesla electricity broadcasting coils, but essentially all electronic devices received their electricity wirelessly. Just like wireless Internet, sometimes the coils required a pass code to access the power.

Patrick was relaying a story to Mr. Drake about nearly totaling his car in the process of trying to impress a girl he picked up. Most highways in New England, although updated, ran along the same old routes from pre-collapse. The main difference were the elevated mag tunnels in the median of each highway, or sometimes right above the road if the median wasn't big enough. The roads were paved in a type of ceramic that was pretty much just mud and clay with different types of common metals added, and heated to firmness while steamrolling. It was cheap to build, drained water, and lasted a long time, especially since traffic was relatively low.

It was a little expensive for access to most roads, but companies sold subscriptions to bundle access if it wasn't included in another service; Mr. Patrick could travel on almost any road in New England for $175 per month. The owners would have the roads patrolled to make sure users had paid for access. A radio frequency transmitter was issued to subscribers so security patrols could receive the signal, and if they did not, drivers would be detained and issued a fine by the road company.

When Mr. Patrick's story about almost killing himself and the girl in a high speed wreck came to a close, and the pair's laughter died down, the conversation turned to the controversy surrounding Atlas Protection, and the ruling which had come out of Barry Arbitration the day before.

"I've already begun picking up customers from the fallout," Patrick told Drake. "Talk about good luck on our part."

"Yes..." Drake drawled with a smirk – his smiles becoming more frequent and noticeable over the last few days. "Quite our *luck*," and he accentuated the word luck while keeping eye contact with Patrick.

After a brief look of bewilderment, understanding came over Patrick's face and he raised his head in an ah-ha sort of manner, before narrowing his eyes and nodding, with a sly smirk of his own.

"And what about Barry? He must know he's going to get screwed sooner rather than later?" Patrick questioned.

Drake sat silent for a moment, deciding how to advance the subject. "Well... Have you ever noticed that our two companies, mine and yours; our contracts cover more than half of the southern and western borders of New England, when you figure in our field offices for response and patrols?"

"Are you saying it doesn't end with Atlas?" Patrick sounded skeptical but was leaning in with keen interest, eyes still narrowed, smirk still visible.

Drake was still smiling. "I own route 90 and 84, you own route 95, 15, and route 1, and up further north there's barely any traffic anyway. So when we are talking about mag tunnel traffic from the New York City area, you and I control 5 out of 8 host roads, and the first pod station in New England for each of the 5 mag tunnels."

"Is there a kicker you're gonna get to?" Patrick asked lightly still smirking. He was rubbing his hands together unconsciously.

Drake laughed, "Well a good gambler wouldn't reveal his hand, but let's just say I've got an ace in the hole and when the smoke clears, you and I are gonna be the house."

Patrick sat back in his seat and looked up toward the ceiling, thinking. He put his hand to his chin, rubbing it while thinking. "I think I catch your drift... but it sounds like we'd be taking a big risk."

Drake nodded, "Yeah, it is a risk. But the less you know, the smaller *your* risk. I just need to know if you're on board when this ship sails."

Patrick was nodding, but still looking past Drake, thinking. He licked his lips, leaned in closer, and looked at Drake.

"Just give me a taste. No details, just the general theme."

"There's a crisis: New England is being inundated with drugs and violence from New York City. We're the saviors."

Patrick smiled wider, and again leaned back in his chair, once again delving into thought, with thin sly eyes, rubbing his shaved chin.

"So I don't need to be in the loop – I don't want to be. I just gotta follow your lead when the shit hits the fan. And I get..." he looked at Drake curiously.

Businessmen love to minimize risk, and maximize return. Patrick was a good businessman; smart, knew how to keep the customers happy, deliver what they wanted, and turn a profit. He was extremely wealthy, even more so than Drake. He had attained the most power this society had to offer, which was economic power.

But in the old days, there was always more power available, beyond economics; in economics you still had to get everyone's agreement in each transaction – you just had an advantage the greater your economic means. But pre-collapse the best way to minimize risk and maximize return was to get the backing of the government – usually to subsidize your business or regulate away a competitor's business.

Here Patrick was, already one benefactor of his strongest competitor's (Atlas Protection's) knee-capping. This sounded like a sure thing: either it works, and he gets power unattainable in a free society, or it fails, and he had nothing to do with it; complete ignorance. No money exchanging hands, no recorded communications, just a deal between businessmen. Drake's benefit was the cavalry riding in for support, and Patrick's incentive was being a foundational brick in the revival of the old power structure: monopolizing force, and initiating it without retaliation. Government.

"How does, Minister of Transportation sound? No one moving about without your permission. Complete control of the air, sea, roads and mag system in all of New England."

"Say no more!" Patrick had practically jumped out of his seat, beaming a smile from ear to ear. "Just give me the signal, and we are good to go."

Drake stood as well, shaking Patrick's hand confidently. "We're looking at about two or three weeks out. I'll be in touch."

Drake planned to escalate the unrest for a few weeks leading up to initiating New England borders. He wanted to have everything in place before he delivered on his promise to Barry. But the timeframe was short; he had to get rid of Molly and her information before the release of BER's report on Barry Arbitration, and while the report was still under Molly's control. Even though Molly usually worked on a shared file accessible via Internet, stored in a cloud, she still had ultimate control over the information and documents until it was ceded to BER for editing and publication. She could delete it all if she wanted to, up until it was due to Business Ethics Review, about a week before the publication.

Drake had just about a week to set it all up before the first domino would fall; the attack on Molly. There were only a handful of people Drake could trust to make sure the public didn't find out about the plan. Obviously Barry already knew, and would become Minister of Arbitration in the new regime; like the top judge. Drake would be Minister of Security which made him Commander in Chief: President. Drake was still playing around with the titles; he couldn't decide if he wanted to be called President, and have his administrators referred to as Vice President of this or that, or to stick with Minister. He thought minister would have a better connotation with the public, but then it might be less clear who was really in charge – something Drake wanted crystal clear after power was solidified and the smoke cleared.

For now he stuck with ministers for the sake of organizing. Mr. Patrick was the third member added to the impending government, as Minister of Transportation. If only Drake could bring the girl from decades ago, to whom his mind so often floated, into the fold. *She would have been a perfect Minister of Education* Drake thought. She really cared, and even when shaping minds in a particular way for a particular outcome, you need someone who cares. She would have agreed with the benefit of keeping certain information from young minds for the sake of the future goals, and focusing on other information to achieve the desired outcome. She had said if a lie was told to produce a better result, then it was justified. Of course that was also what lead to her untimely death in the mid 2080's.

Drake's fiance had decided to prepare for a career in education by traveling to other developing areas of the globe in order to introduce people to the New England Style Economy: natural, free market based organization of society. The New England Economy was introduced first by Food Corp after they expanded beyond their walls, and ushered in the New England Renaissance, which preceded the current worldwide Modern Renaissance by more than 70 years.

But the problem was, a lot of these foreign places would not accept the new system: they couldn't get past the idea that no one would be in charge. For some it was self interest; they rejected the system because they were currently big fish in small ponds. Small backwards ponds with lots of violence and poverty, only slightly improved from the New Dark Ages, which did not give way worldwide until the early 2080's. Others were confused by the idea of economic transactions being the basis for law, since law was considered more important than profits. Though they put up with daily injustices, it was still somehow assumed that the injustices would be even greater if the market were to provide for people's security and punish victimizers.

So the young woman that Drake loved misled the parents of these foreign children into thinking she was only teaching their kids basic skills to improve the economic situation in the area, without changing the system. She indeed did teach them math, science, reading, writing, and history. But she didn't stop there. The love of Drake's life developed strategies to teach the students to question authority, to never trust those with inherently unequal power. She taught them that all force was immoral, unless in response to force initiated against an individual. Though there was merit in teaching these things, she betrayed her own philosophy by misleading parents about what she would be teaching their children. She misrepresented her goals in order to gain access to the young minds, to transition the society away from a repressive state. To her the ends, a better society, justified the means, forcing her views on a captive audience, against the will of the audience's guardians.

When the parents inevitably found out what she had been teaching their children, they were furious, and immediately alerted the local government to what was happening. She was arrested by the Chief, and all of her cohorts were thrown out of the small chiefdom. A kangaroo court tried her case, and delivered a guilty verdict in a matter of hours. She was sentenced to death by stoning, the sentence carried out later the same day that the verdict was delivered.

The local government responded so harshly because some of the parents supported what she taught, and this created a rift in the community. Coming out of the New Dark Ages, death was not a big deal to these people, they had grown desensitized to murder.

It happened too quickly for anyone outside the country to respond – by the time they contacted the Chiefdom leaders to appeal for her release, she had been dead 48 hours, and left in the center of the capital to decompose. Her body was recovered however, and Drake identified it upon its return to New England. That was an image and a smell, he would never be able to erase from his brain. The love of his life, taken from him, mutilated, dishonored in death, all while performing a task Drake himself had convinced her to take on. From that moment on, Drake was filled with, and handicapped by, regret.

Even thirty years later, he was not at peace, he would never be. Drake considered what happened to his lost love an indication of human nature, leading to his belief that it was justified for a "better" person to control others who could not be trusted to do the right thing. It was lost on Drake that it was precisely those people who controlled others that carried out the murder of his fiancée. *People are bad*, he thought, *and need to be controlled*; he ignored the fact that only "other people" could control them, thus not solving the original problem that "people are bad."

Drake guessed – incorrectly – that his fiancée would have gone along with his plan if he could convince her of the benefits. This was however somewhat circular thinking; Drake probably never would have desired this type of power if he had the girl he loved to go home to every night. And even though Drake may have thought otherwise, his fiancée would *never* have helped Drake rip control away from the people. She had died for the ideal of sovereign individuals; she had given her life in the pursuit of abolition of all slavery, in all its forms, even if she had compromised her principles in doing so.

The buzz from his secretary ripped Drake out of his reminiscing about his lost love and back into reality. A woman was waiting for a meeting Drake had arranged with her. He would be selling her the position of Minister of Resources, since her company supplied power to almost 7% of New England, the largest share of any other company.

She and Drake went way back. He once "lost" a file on some wrongdoing while her company was being established, and in turn she strategically cut the power to a well-positioned NESA competitor during their grand opening week, giving the impression of incompetence and helping to stunt their growth. Drake knew she was open to trades beyond strictly economic transactions.

By the time she left his office, the future administration had grown one woman stronger. Drake now had the ability to strategically cut power if need be to a couple hundred thousand people and businesses, almost 10,000 of whom were located within three miles of the future New England border. The woman left the office beaming and energetic, ready to put things in place for the plan to be carried out. Drake sat back in his chair, growing more confident by the day.

Trix was eating at Hillside. He had gotten some stares from people who could detect the nuances of wealthy versus poor, but most people were sufficiently tricked by his new clothes. He had arrived a bit high, but immediately tipped the waiter well before his meal even started so that he would get good service, calming any nervousness the waiter would have about the ability of some unrecognized high guy to pay his bill.

Hillside was not simply a restaurant, but an entire venue, an atmosphere. It was built on the peak of a hill that on the east overlooked a long lake, on the west a small valley. It was only a five minute pod ride from the main metropolitan area surrounding Food Corp, which roughly corresponded with where Worcester used to be. People would come from all over New England – and often further – for a night at Hillside. Many of the natural rocks were left in place on the west side, with tables and artificial decorations added. In good weather the entire west veranda, called the Peppercorn Patio, would be left open to the elements and diners would enjoy the sunset with their meals, or they could dine at the Hillside bar, Cliffhanger. Glass walls and ceilings waited to be activated, individually, or all together forming a giant indoor greenhouse. But even when it was indoors, the natural rocks and plants remained. This helped keep spirits up during the long New England winter.

On the east side, steps, patios and porches twisted their way down the hill to the water. Patrons could take a stroll down to the edge and onto the dock, where there was another bar on the water. About halfway up the east hill was the Hillside club for the younger crowd that wanted to dance and party. It was mostly glass with the large floor stretching out over the hill to form a plateau. It was a sight to see at night from on the lake, the three story glass building shimmering with lasers and flashing lights of all colors, seeming to pulse with the beat of the music. Fog often poured out of the club, sliding slowly down the hill, illuminated by lasers, and tumbling onto the glassy surface of the lake.

A large tower stood on the peak of the hill, offering another restaurant with a different menu. Above the restaurant were rooms with more bars, and different themes, as well as various tower lookouts. Rooms in this tower rented for no less than $2,500 per night, and the penthouse was $12,000 per night in the off-season. Hillside was arguably New England's most popular and most exclusive venue.

Vast gardens and paths surrounded the compound providing a lush environment for a romantic getaway, or a drunken stroll. There were always little nooks and crannies in which to escape – a spiral stone staircase covered in vines lead to a heart shaped wooden bench surrounded by 10 foot high perfectly manicured hedges, embedded with twinkling lights. A camouflaged cavern, cool and echoing, with a sunken-in couch set in the center of the natural cave, illuminated by a medieval cast iron chandelier.

Turn a corner and there might be another little half-building, offering a dartboard and pool table. Another twist, around a boulder, up a flight of stairs and a large hot tub awaited bubbling, the edge seeming to disappear off the cliff, with a perfect view of the night sky, and shimmering stars. Hillside was not too concerned if you brought your bathing suit; in designated areas patrons could feel free to strip down and go for a swim or soak in a tub au naturel.

Trix sat in the semi-indoor section of Peppercorn Patio on the west terrace of the hill, overlooking the valley, speckled with brightly colored leaves of orange, yellow, and red. It was not cold, but a crisp autumn day, therefore large Persian-style torches provided extra warmth. The first course Trix managed to get through without thinking much: New England clam chowder with a side of crab cakes. But as the second course arrived and he cut into a juicy steak, grief overcame Trix; his impending assignment weighing heavy on him.

Trix was not a violent person, he simply didn't have a very structured upbringing. His mom and dad both worked long hours picking crops and tending farmers' fields when he was younger, so he didn't have much direction. When they got home from work, they were too tired to do much parenting, though they truly did love their son.

His dad died when he was 12 from a complication brought on by a bullet he took during the New Dark Ages. His dad was born in the "Kingdom" which arose out of Georgia after the collapse. It was a poorer region when his dad was born, just beginning to integrate with New England and the New England Style Economy. His dad had gotten into it with a gang, though shortly afterward, the gang was taken out by Royal Liberty, the former non-coercive "Monarchs" of the southern Atlantic coast, turned security company after integration with New England.

When Trix's dad died, he had even less supervision going into his teenage years. Trix kept busy hanging out with the kids of the other farmhands who mostly lived on the same crowded dead end street in small shacks. He would seek thrills riding his bicycle off jumps and through shallow rivers, playing chicken or jousting on his bike with the other neighborhood kids, or seeing how high he could climb in a tree or up a rock face. They would climb on top of the larger farm animals and see how far they could surf before face-planting in the mud.

Of course, as he got older this just escalated to seeing how fast he could drive his car around dangerous curves, and partying all night with less reputable types. That's where he started trying various drugs, which was the next best thrill he could get.

After Trix moved out of his mom's house on a whim with a girl that didn't stick around, he floated here and there traveling, and working for UtopaCorp before ending up in New England because he heard they had the best quality adaps.

Now here he was, eating at the best restaurant he had ever entered, wearing clothes that cost 10 times as much as the next best thing he had ever worn, buying more sophisticated and refined drugs, and he could not be more miserable. Trix wracked his brain for a way out of killing Molly; it didn't help that he was often too high for his brain to function properly.

Maybe I'll find my mom and move back down south, try to find some work or a decent adap, he thought. *But they would surely find me. What if I changed my name and went to work for UtopaCorp again? They provide security, and I could save up to buy a gun for good measure. And then what? Run for the rest of my life? Anyway I would have to be mostly clean before going to work for UtopaCorp, and that would take longer than the handful of days left before I'm supposed to kill Molly.*

Trix put his head down on the table distressed, eliciting some concerned glances from other diners.

"Sir, is everything alright?" asked the stately waiter with his hands behind his back and a gently furrowed brow.

Trix looked up with sunken eyes plagued by redness and shadows.

"Yeah I'm fine, but I could use another," he held up his almost empty glass twirling the remnants a bit before finishing the cocktail and placing it back down lightly.

"Of course, sir. Right away."

Trix stared out the large open windows over the valley. Where could he go, what could he do to disappear? There was nowhere he could go that the agents couldn't go more easily. He thought about alternative societies where he might be able to blend in, and find some strength in numbers. But the communist ones generally encouraged new people to contribute what they have to the group... and Trix didn't have much. He had some money, but he didn't want to hand that over to the collective, only to be left high and dry a month later. Anyway, they did not so much approve of the types of drugs Trix did, preferring hallucinogens and psychedelics over amphetamines and narcotics.

There were non-communist alternatives, but they were pay to play. You either had to have a marketable skill, be willing to learn one, or have enough resources already that you would not be dragging the group down in these societal microcosms. And they were hard to get into without knowing someone... and again, the drug habit posed a problem.

Trix decided the best course of action was to head to the bathroom to take another hit, at least that way he would be able to enjoy what time he had left to spend at Hillside. When he got back, the waiter pretended not to notice Trix nodding off a couple times, before ordering more food and drink. An hour later Trix paid his bill, grabbed one more cocktail, and stumbled off down the west slope to see where the paths would take him.

Barry was back and forth, nervous then excited, terrified then elated about the impending plan for power. He wanted it so badly, but it so terrified him. He couldn't sleep, so he got out of bed slowly as not to wake... *what was her name again?* Barry thought. He had to picture his bank account statement to remember. *She costs me the most of any of them. Lisa? It starts with an L. Lily!*

After splashing some water on his face, Barry stared into the bathroom mirror. In the back of his mind Barry was irked by the thought that if he was smarter in his younger years, if he hadn't been so cocky, he could have retired already and just collected enough profits from the business to live better than any King had ever lived, quite literally.

But he loved the power of his position when he first started his company and it took off. With every heartbeat the feeling of superiority had coursed through his veins. It invaded his brain like a drug; pride radiated from his pores. He couldn't take it when another up-and-comer made a joke at an "important" social gathering. The boy didn't even mean it derisively, he actually thought it would be taken lightly. Barry struggled to remember what the jab was even about. He remembered the two had been acquaintances – the other probably thought they were friends.

Perhaps it was a tease about his appearance, or a quip about someone Barry had been seen taking out on the town. But it made Barry hate him with a passion. From that day on, everything this young man said made Barry burn with rage. He used Barry's first name, Reed; showed no respect at all, despite the fact that Barry had built his business, while this boy merely got a job in the same field at a relative's firm.

It required substantial effort for Barry to take revenge on the supposed wrongs suffered. In those days a pleasant social life was just beginning to re-emerge as normal, and people like Barry sucked down popularity like gluttons at a feast.

It took social maneuvering, a great deal of charisma, and plenty of backhanded planning. But months later, long after the culprit had forgotten about the party at which he "wronged" Mr. Barry, the boy was fired from his relative's company. Barry was happy for his absence at that year's social gatherings, but much to Barry's chagrin the young man was back the next year, having started his own company.

By now he knew that Mr. Barry had been the catalyst behind his firing, and gave Mr. Barry a smug welcome, flaunting his resilience to Barry's slander. The boy thanked Barry for allowing him the opportunity to start his own business, and elevating him to a place he could not have gotten employed at the old firm.

And of course, the people Barry had manipulated into sacking the young man had also learned by now of Barry's dishonesty. This made certain company interactions tough, and any business at all with that particular young man and his contacts impossible. Had Barry known what the man would become, he would have avoided slighting him at all costs. However had Barry not pulled the strings of the young man's firing, the boy may never have risen to that level in the first place.

It would be many more years of Barry Arbitration earning its somewhat sketchy reputation, but that was the beginning. Funny that such a petty action by Barry had reverberated so deeply in his life. Barry knew that had he been more humble, he would have no worries. But he had learned too much from the pre-collapse ways of the world – not that he remembered, but from what he read. These days a solid network and friendly relations were as good as gold, and dishonesty was a cancer on business which good people would not abide.

This is an opportunity, Barry finally decided. The redemption he needed to remedy the stupidity of his youth. *Drastic times call for drastic measures, and I brought this on myself. Instead of sitting back at this point in my life, I am forced to undertake the most dangerous and risky endeavor yet*. He was scared, but his mind was made up. There was no calling off the plan. Mr. Barry would become Minister Barry, head of the Department of Arbitration, or he would die trying.

Six

It was the date and time that was specified on the envelope. Trix took a pod to the neighborhood where Molly lived, but got off at an earlier stop to walk. He had traveled in a pattern that made it hard to track his movements with the various security recordings that people and businesses ran. He traveled to a gap with no surveillance, and came out of it with his face obscured by his sweatshirt, hood, and makeup that would make facial recognition harder.

He was dreading what he had to do, but what choice did he have? It was either kill Molly, or be killed by the agents. Trix could not stop thinking about this deed every second as it drew nearer. He had considered taking the money and hiring security to protect him, but he was not convinced they would be able to. Agent White and Agent Orange could just wait until he ran out of money, and then come after him. He considered how they would be able to find him, but knew what kind of technology they had at their disposal. Trix also would not even know how to describe the agents, or who they worked for, or if a security company would even be interested in taking the risk to protect him.

Each of the past five days Trix had ordered a pod, and almost entered a distant location. But in the end he always took the pod to a nice restaurant or a shopping mall, or to buy more and better drugs. In the week since Trix received the payment he had blown through $4,500 worth of the Atlantitrade currency. Part of this was due to his impulsive personality and drug addiction, but trying to distract himself from the job at hand was another big piece of it. Here he was, caught between a rock and a hard place, knowing that he would never be able to get rid of the guilt of performing this task.

Trix had bought a special mixture of drugs for this, to numb him to what he was about to do. He had also bought a number of drugs for afterward, to numb him to what he had done.

Walking through the neighborhood, a few blocks away from the address, Trix popped two pills which had similar effects to cocaine and pcp, but added an aloof downer effect that made him ambivalent but didn't cause much disorientation. One block later and he felt like he was in a video game; another block and he couldn't even remember what guilt felt like; just one block away he felt like a ninja assassin in a blockbuster movie who was about to fulfill his righteous destiny, before escaping to distant lands where he would have girls, wealth, and glory.

The plan was in his head; he had sketched it out before, thought about each step, and was now envisioning a to-do list of tasks to accomplish his mission. Mission: now he felt like an old world secret agent, infiltrating an enemy data center and taking out a destructive target.

Trix briefly looked to see if Molly had any video surveillance out front, and it didn't look like she did. He walked up to her door, and rang the doorbell, and stepped back.

Molly was working on her laptop in the living room with her TV on. She wasn't expecting anyone, but didn't think it was too strange for someone to stop by at this time; it was still before 21:00 and a weekend. Molly was typically engrossed in her work, even though she didn't really have to be. But she enjoyed it, and was scrutinizing the details in Barry Arbitration's review. Just one more piece and she could downgrade BA according to Business Ethics Review standards. She had looked over the same information multiple times, making tables, diagrams, and graphs to try to see some piece she hadn't seen before. There were certainly dead ends, but every time she looked over the reports, she found another piece of the puzzle.

Molly figured maybe some neighborhood kid was selling something, or maybe a group was organizing a boycott, or maybe one of her friends was in the neighborhood and decided to stop by. She didn't recognize the man standing on her front porch, but he didn't look particularly threatening. It was typical of someone Molly's age to let their guard down – she had only ever known a peaceful society where justice flourished.

Violence was not something on the forefront of the mind of anyone under 40, though more seasoned folks remembered periods of unrest much more clearly. It was partly due to the older generation's use of self defense and refusal to be victimized that aggression had taken a long and steady nosedive over the last 60 years. Violence had reached its modern pinnacle during the New Dark Ages, the years following the collapse in the 2020's. Only once organizations to protect individuals' rights rose up out of demand was this trend curbed.

The first such company to form policing and protection agencies after the collapse was Food Corp, which was the biggest societal element leftover in New England. In fact, only a handful of communities with some semblance of law and order existed in North America for decades after the collapse.

Of course the New Dark Ages were not on Molly's mind as she opened the door. Trix was smiling warmly as he kicked the door just as Molly began to open it, slamming the heavy oak into her left foot, which broke three of her toes, and toppled her onto the floor. As she screamed out in pain and horror, Trix quickly stepped inside and shut and locked the door. He very calmly and methodically bent down and grabbed Molly's throat to stop her from screaming.

"Be quiet, and I won't hurt you anymore," he said in monotone as he let go of Molly's throat.

She coughed and sucked in air, trying to catch her breath, hyperventilating from the pain and shock. Tears streaming down her face, Molly looked up at Trix terrified, and rapidly nodded her head in agreement, unable to speak.

"All I want is your cash and jewelry. Anything valuable."

Even when Trix looked at Molly there was nothing behind his eyes. It was like he was staring at a boring slide show presentation, trying to maintain focus. Trix grabbed one of Molly arms and yanked her to her feet. She let out a short cry as some weight shifted to her broken toes, but quickly bit her lip to silence herself.

Trix removed a small black knife from his pocket, and made a "shh" gesture, putting the blade up to his lips in place of his finger. As he did this, he couldn't help but let out a giggle, amused at his use of the knife in shushing Molly. He felt like he was in a dream, and this task was playing out easier than he thought. It was the drugs.

Molly began to lead him into her bedroom where she kept a safe, and as they crossed the living room Trix grabbed her foldable tablet, and put it into his backpack.

Molly thought it was strange that the man who had just kicked in her door was taking a year old tablet without much value, but she was still too scared to speak. Molly desperately hoped that the man would just take what he came for and leave; his eyes said he was on a mission. In her bedroom she opened her closet door and unlocked the safe.

Trix was rummaging through drawers and her desk. He found a flash drive in her bureau and a tablet was sitting on her bedside table, both went into his backpack. When Trix heard the click of the safe unlocking, he quickly sprang over to it and put his hand on the door to stop Molly from opening it herself. Nudging her out of the way, Trix went into the safe, took an external hard drive that was connected wirelessly to the rest of the electronics in the house, and also stole the little amount of jewelry – a couple silver coins and one antique looking golden coin.

Molly also had a handgun in her safe which her dad had given her. She wasn't really interested in guns, but he had insisted that she take it to be safe. She wished that she had kept the gun out in her living room, or at least concealed and accessible, but the chances of something like this happening were so small that there was no way for her to predict it.

Trix took the handgun, and cocked it. Molly let out a gasp and quickly covered her mouth, but Trix tucked the handgun into his pants.

"Show me the rest of your electronics," Trix said, without expression. Even when his eyes met Molly, it was like she was not even in front of him. She noticed this too, that his eyes seemed to look through her, focused on nothing in her room.

"There's... the TV in the living room... and another tablet in the kitchen... and a telescreen in the living room and kitchen." Her voice was trembling, cracking every few words, with tears still running down her cheeks, and hiccups interrupting her speech.

It seemed like Trix was almost taken out of his trance for a moment, but he quickly turned away, about to leave the room, the drugs still suppressing his emotions.

Walking through the living room to the kitchen, Trix noticed an open window, as it was an unusually warm fall night. Trix closed the window. Molly all of a sudden felt like she couldn't breathe. She was panicking, but she was so frightened and her mind was in such knots that she couldn't pinpoint why.

"Please... please don't hurt me," Molly choked out between sobs.

"I told you I just want the valuables," Trix restated emotionless.

Molly shot a glance towards the window. There was no reason for this intruder to close the window if he intended to leave after pillaging the rest of her electronics. Trix had taken the rest of the electronics and put them into his backpack. The only ones he couldn't take were the telescreens attached to the living room wall and kitchen counter.

Trix pointed at the kitchen counter telescreen. "Log in."

Molly swallowed hard, and did as she was told. Trix then pushed her aside, and started opening up various accounts, and deleting the contents. He opened the cloud storage, and purged it. He had to click multiple warnings about deleting information permanently. Then he had to go into the deleted files section, and purge those permanently. He went through this process on at least three different accounts, changing the password and email on each account when he was done. Molly was feeling sicker and sicker, not being able to explain why this supposed thief was interested in deleting her information if all he wanted was money and valuables.

She kept glancing into the living room to the panic button 15 or so feet away. She was too terrified to make the leap however, and was distracted by her feelings of terror that this was more than a robbery.

"And your portable," Trix said, indicating that he wanted Molly's pocket sized tablet. She walked into the living room to retrieve her mini-tab on a couch-side table. Turning around she tried not to glance once again at the panic button, and gave her mini-tab to Trix. She was now only two steps from the wall mounted panic button.

"Okay," Trix said, but didn't move. He glanced at the door, he glanced at the window he had closed, and he briefly looked back at Molly. "Okay," he repeated monotonously.

Molly was staring at him, frozen with fear, praying to whatever god might be listening that he would just leave. Trix's hand shot down towards the gun in his waistband, like a cowboy drawing in a duel. In one swift motion he had raised the gun pointing it directly at Molly's face, as she turned sideways and squinted, bursting into a renewed fit of tears. He was only three feet away from Molly, the gun closer, squared at her temple; he pulled the trigger.

The moment the trigger was pulled felt like an eternity to Molly, the fall of the hammer seeming to span meters. She had time to reopen her eyes, and look back towards Trix through her tears, down the barrel of the gun. She could see the rifled grooves of the cylinder, and as she blinked, she swore she saw her life flash before her eyes. By the time her eyes opened the trigger was pulled. She expected to hear a loud boom, see a bright flash, and have everything go dark. Instead she heard a click.

It took her a split second to remember that the pistol her father had given her was coded to her DNA, so that no one but she could fire it. Trix evidently had not realized this, because he turned the gun sideways, examining the slide to see what could have caused the misfire. Molly knew she had to seize this opportunity before he found some other way to kill her, like the knife he brought, but she didn't think she would be strong enough to wrestle the gun from him. She launched towards the telescreen in the living room, flipped open the clear plastic hatch above the screen to the right, and slammed down the red button with a force sure to bruise her palm, then immediately thrust herself toward her bedroom, ignoring the searing pain in her broken toes.

By the time Trix realized what happened, and raced to pursue Molly, she was in her bedroom with the door slammed shut, locked. Molly then ran into the master bathroom, slamming and locking that door as well. She immediately started frantically searching the room for anything that could be used as a weapon to protect herself. It would be just a matter of minutes until police arrived.

Trix slammed into Molly's door with full force. He pounded on it with both fists, and hysterically twisted the knob trying desperately to open the door. Trix backed up, and put his full force and weight, shoulder first, into the door. It rattled but didn't budge. He again looked at the gun in his hand, trying to figure out how to make it shoot, but abandoned that idea quickly, placing it back in his waist band.

Looking around the room he searched for something that could be used as a battering ram, but his time was running out. He picked up a heavy stone statue of Buddha, and slammed the base into the door handle to Molly's room. The first time the handle cracked. The second time a small Buddha shaped hole appeared in the door. On the third try, the bedroom door burst open, spraying splinters of wood onto the floor.

In the bathroom Molly heard the crash and began to sob harder, on her knees rifling through everything under the sink, still searching for the proper weapon. The scissors in her bathroom were too small to be an effective defense. There were no blunt objects, and no sharp objects long enough to do any kind of serious damage. She heard Trix slamming something heavy into the bathroom door.

Molly shot to her feet with a spray can of room fragrance, and as the door busted open and Trix rushed in, Molly sprayed the aerosol can of perfume directly into his eyes. Trix let out a loud scream of agony as the liquid burned his eyes. He stumbled back against the wall dropping the Buddha statue onto the bathroom floor, rubbing violently at his eyes. He tried to open his eyes, but it burned more, and he could only make out the outline of Molly. Trix lunged to block the bathroom door so that she had no escape route. He could hear the sirens, they couldn't be more than 5 blocks away, and rapidly closing in.

Molly, seeing her exit blocked, opened the medicine cabinet mirror with full force, slamming it against the wall, and shattering it into pieces. With no time to spare, she grabbed the largest shard she could find, and raised it towards Trix.

Trix heard the shattering of the glass, and the sirens getting closer, but he could still only see in outlines and blurs. As Molly brought the shard of glass down towards Trix, he managed to turn towards the bathroom door, and the sharp piece of glass only grazed his back before ripping into his backpack, filled with the stolen electronics. Molly let out a sharp cry of pain as the glass shard she gripped penetrated deep into her palm. She let go and pulled her hand back, seeing blood spraying out with each beat of her heart.

She watched Trix flee out into the bedroom, and turn running into the living room. Molly sunk down onto the floor of her bathroom, and coddled her severely lacerated hand that was spurting blood, already pooling on the floor, and soaking her shorts. The sirens sounded like they were right outside now, and relief started to pour over her. Molly's sobs were now a hysterical mix of terror, pain, and happiness upon the arrival of the police.

Trix was stumbling through the living room trying to see where he was going. He saw the bright lights of the cop cars coming through the front windows, and heard the slam of their car doors. He moved as quickly as he could through the kitchen to the back door, bumping hard against the counter on the way. He managed to open the sliding glass door, and escape onto the back porch as he heard Molly's front door burst open as the police broke it down with a battering ram. He was past the bushes running through the neighbor's lawn by the time another officer came running around the house, and saw the open sliding door.

"We need dogs! Get the Canine units!" The officer's voice was clear and loud.

As he barked the order, Trix could hear it clearly from the next street that he was now fleeing down. He saw headlights coming around the corner, and took a left turn down another road in the neighborhood to avoid the car. His sight was returning, though his eyes still burned red. Looking over his shoulder, Trix could see a skyship approaching where Molly's house must have been. He couldn't tell if it was a medical unit or a police unit. Trix was sprinting down the center of the road, when an SUV came around the corner toward him, and screeched to a halt.

Rolling down the window, the man behind the wheel who looked in his late 60's yelled at Trix, "What the hell do you think you're doing?! I almost hit you, you could have been-" He was cut off by Trix's deep gutted yell, as Trix grabbed the gun out of his waistband, hoping the man would follow his orders, since the gun would not fire.

"Get out of the car!" The drugs were still in his system, but emotion could finally be heard in his voice, though it manifested more as anger than fear on Trix's part. Instead of exiting his vehicle the man inside seemed to duck down, avoiding the path of the gun, while pressing a button that raised the window.

"I SAID-" Trix grabbed the door handle, but it was locked, so he slammed the window with the butt end of his handgun, shattering it in a spider web form, though the pieces stayed in place ."".GET. OU-"

BAM! The glass flew out of the car, spraying all over the street. BAM! BAM! Two more shots rang out from inside the vehicle. Trix was still standing, but began to stumble back, feeling immediately lightheaded and more confused than the drugs could account for. He looked down at his body to see two large blood stains spreading on his shirt, and blood squirting out from what must have been his neck. As black closed in from the sides of his eyes, he tried to maintain balance. The older man from the car opened the door, and exited the vehicle with his gun still trained on Trix, but all Trix saw were swirling outlines as the world seemed to turn around him.

The brand new medical nanobots coursing through Trix's bloodstream rushed to the areas of trauma, frantically attempting to stymie the blood flow, and repair the tissue, but the damage was too great.

Trix was somehow still standing but his face was blank as his useless gun slipped from his hand, and clinked onto the street. As the life left Trix's eyes he took one final step back before his knee buckled, and he fell backwards. Feebly, Trix twitched his right arm in a final attempt to grasp something, and his limp body slammed onto the pavement like a bag of meat, mouth agape, eyes still open, as emotionless as ever.

Molly was a customer of Corner Cop Security, and it was Officer Themis who came to her hospital bed to take her statement and begin gathering evidence for the CCS investigation into the break-in. Being the lead investigator for violent crimes for Corner Cop Security, Themis would not be patrolling until this case was fully investigated and resolved.

Molly's hand and foot had been bandaged, and it was now getting close to midnight.

"Hi Molly, my name is Officer Themis. I know it is tough, but I need to take a statement from you about the break-in."

Molly understood, took a deep breath, and did her best to describe what happened in detail.

"...And the whole time I just kept thinking, he's not here to rob me. He took all my computer devices, and he grabbed some stuff out of the safe, but he didn't even seem to care about the coins or cash. It was like he was there specifically for my devices. And..." Molly brought her hand to her mouth to suppress the desire to start crying again. "And I don't know why he kept coming after me, once he had everything. It doesn't make any sense." She sniffled and a tear rolled down her cheek. Themis was writing this all down on his tablet. "Did they catch him?" Molly asked.

"Oh I thought someone told you. He tried to steal a car a couple blocks from your house. The car owner shot him in the process. He's dead. His name was Trix, he's a drug addict from uptown. Honestly I can't believe it myself, I knew him and this is totally uncharacteristic. We're probing to see if this goes deeper."

"Deeper?" Molly questioned.

"Well, it's standard; we just want to make sure it's an isolated event. We have seen people do things before when they are desperate for money. Good thing he didn't make off with all your AtlantiTrade notes. We recovered them with the rest of the stuff he took, you'll get it back within a few days once it has been processed for evidence. You must have worked a while to save those."

Molly shook her head, looking confused, and after a couple seconds stated, "But I didn't have any AtlantiTrade notes."

Themis likewise wore a befuddled look momentarily, and made a note on his tablet.

Just then his portable chimed in his pocket to indicate he was getting a call. "Excuse me for a sec. Hello... yes... what, why?... Okay... Okay... try to find an arbiter who will reverse the decision. Thanks, let me know when you get the warrant."

"What happened?" Molly asked concerned.

"Well, we subpoenaed the video records of Trix's adap, but they were blocked."

"Why? Isn't that standard in an investigation, why wouldn't the building owners give up the footage?"

"It wasn't the owners who blocked it, it was the arbiter that their security company uses, Barry Arbitration."

"WHAT?!" Molly practically jumped out of bed, startling Officer Themis.

"You know them?" he asked, eyes wide, eyebrows raised. "Kind of gained a sleazier reputation the last couple years."

"I'm in the process of reviewing BA. They were going to get downgraded, but almost everything I had was-" Molly stopped abruptly and turned pale.

"Was what?" asked Themis, concerned.

"It was all on my devices that were taken," Molly said quietly and slowly without looking at Themis.

Themis didn't want to believe that an arbitration agency would attempt to kill a reporter in order to bury a bad rating, but it *was* strange that the subpoena was blocked, and it did seem coincidental that it was blocked by the same agency Molly was investigating.

"We're going to get to the bottom of this, Molly. I will personally see to it. Until then, CCS will have someone posted outside your room. Try to get some rest."

Molly managed to squeeze out a feeble "Thanks."

As Themis left the hospital, he ordered a tail on Barry, just to cover all the bases.

The next morning Themis decided to drive over to Trix's adap himself to check it out, and hoped that while he was there looking through Trix's apartment, a warrant would be approved by a different arbitration agency for the surveillance records. On the ride over, the speakers were playing a segment about last night's break-in, as crimes of that nature were pretty rare. It was a replay from a live report done the night before, with an attractive woman reporting at the scene.

"The intruder was a known drug addict who appeared to be motivated by his desire to get money to pay for drugs, but why he chose that house, no one knows. One theory is that it was a random act of violence, triggered by a specific mixture of drugs, manufactured in New York City, and distributed by a drug cartel, known to operate in the downtown haven. Here with me is the man who eventually ended the spree of the drug addict known as Trix, after an attempted carjacking. What can you tell us about this tragic event?"

"Well, I told those cops that showed up, I didn't know his gun wasn't working, all I knew was he was aiming it at me and trying to get my car. Well you young folks might not get it, but I still carry my old .38 on me. People think it's stupid, but they don't remember the days when people had to use 'em! All you younger folks take this peace for granted, but it hasn't been this way for too long! No sir, I was born just after Food Corp started taking clients outside of their walls, and even then a lot of crimes went unsolved. So how did people deal? Well I'll tell ya, they shot those sons of bitches down on the spot, and why not? You've probably never been hungry in your life, I mean HUNGRY, but I can remember having nothing more than a few berries, and some foraged cattails all day; someone tries to take *that* from you and it's life or death. Sure, I feel bad here, but I did what I had to do; like I said he was pointing a gun at me! And those officers did their job you know, they can't be everywhere, it's not their fault. They came running up just after it happened – quick response – and..."

Themis arrived at the adap with some stares from people on the streets; there weren't too many cars that drove to this area of the city. Themis parked on the side of the road next to the building, and almost bumped into a couple of well-dressed men in suits with sunglasses as he exited his vehicle. He had to do a double take since they were a little too well dressed for this area of town, and it wasn't particularly sunny either.

Barry Arbitration had approved the warrant to search Trix's apartment, but their rationale for nixing the footage subpoena was that it was not targeted enough, and could incriminate innocent people that live in the adaps. This seemed more like an excuse to Themis, since there was practically no arbitration history of using evidence from one crime to open a case on an unrelated crime.

As Themis walked through the entrance to the building, screens in the wide hallway lit up one by one as he walked, with advertisements aimed specifically at Themis; facial recognition was used by advertisers to save money by tailoring ads to certain types of people.

"The latest poly-melding-elastomer vest from Wilderness Gear will stop an animal bite as easy as it will stop a bullet. Lightweight and versatile..."

"This Sunday, live from the Boston Bay Arena, World Obstacle Champion Leon Green will face off against..."

"Are you getting enough potassium, and other essential metals in your diet? Research has shown that as we age..."

Themis brushed past the advertisements and climbed the stairs to Trix's second floor apartment. Themis scanned his card – it opened Trix's door since the warrant had been issued, and access granted to Corner Cop Security. Themis felt a pang of sadness as he gazed around the depressing and filthy room that

Trix formerly inhabited. The mattress was bare though some once white sheets were bunched up in the corner between the bed and the wall. Ads had been disabled until a new tenant was found. The trash overflowed with the wrappers of the worst kinds of foods. The sink had dirty water stuck in it, blocked by the food scraps left at the bottom of the sink. Themis wondered what he even thought he would find here.

Walking aimlessly around the room, Themis tried to separate his feelings from the investigation. It depressed him to think that Trix was a wanna-be murderer, and it just did not seem to fit his personality. Almost unconsciously, Themis nudged the bed with his foot to straighten it out and make it parallel with the wall – to add some tiny bit of order to this dishevelled place. When the mattress moved, he saw a currency note sticking out from under the bed. Picking it up, he realized the note was AtlantiTrade, the same ones found in Trix's possession when he was shot. This showed Themis that Trix hadn't stolen the currency from another victim, at least not the same night. But no major theft of that magnitude had been reported in the area recently either.

What the hell was Trix doing with such a high-valued currency, he thought? And if he had this much money nonchalantly misplaced under his mattress, why would he try to rob someone's house? The drugs could account for some odd behavior, but it still seemed out of place to plan a robbery before even looking through your own apartment for misplaced notes. Themis placed the note into a clear baggy as evidence.

Before leaving Themis scanned some surfaces with a device that detected DNA. While there was plenty of Trix's DNA on the bed and counter, there was no DNA on the wall receiver and none on the doorknob, as if they had been wiped clean. Themis cocked his head and squinted, thinking of an explanation for this, but a dark feeling came over him as things were beginning to look more sinister.

Just then his portable rang, it was someone from the CCS office. They had their warrant, though it took some tricky maneuvering since arbiters were wary of going against another agency's ruling. If Barry Arbitration's reputation had not suffered over the past couple of years, Corner Cop Security probably would have never gotten the warrant for the video surveillance.

Themis walked downstairs and through the wide hallway, bombarded by more ads, and made his way to the building's security office with no windows, set in the center of the building, filled with screens that gave the room a dull glow. Themis showed his credentials, and began to download the video surveillance from the past month, but a chime went off indicating that the footage had been tampered with.

"Why is there an hour missing from the 28th, and an hour missing from this morning?" Themis asked the security manager. He was a balding man with a large stomach and hardened demeanor. He had a scruffy voice, and scruff on his face. He smelt like cigarettes, and Themis wasn't sure if the smell of beer was on his clothes from the night before, or on his breath.

"I couldn't tell you," the manager said hoarsely but loudly, with a hint of attitude.

"Has anyone else been in this office today?" asked Themis sternly.

"I took over at 5:00 this morning. Since then, just me." Themis just stared judgingly, and the security manager looked away apathetically, trying to make it look like he had something else to do.

Yet another piece of the puzzle not fitting together, Themis thought. Themis went outside to his car and turned on the telescreen inside; he was going to make some calls and see if he could get a warrant to search the security manager. If he was the only one in that room since 5:00, and the second hour of footage was missing from 7-8:00, then he must have had something to do with it.

"But what do you expect to find, sir? Even if he did have something to do with it, what would be on his person that would serve as evidence?"

"There is no reason for him to want that footage deleted, it has got to be someone else, so I might find evidence of a third party influence."

The arbiter on the screen shrugged, "Alright let me put in the call, I'll get right back to you."

The arbiter had to make her case to the manager's security company before they would agree to allow the search against one of their clients. A few minutes later Themis got the call that the warrant was approved. He walked back into the security manager's office and showed him the warrant. The manager reluctantly emptied his pockets, and handed over his portable, which Themis had gained permission to search only the last 12 hours of communications.

"I'm gonna have to make a call to my security company," the security manager was saying gruffly, obviously angry about the search. "Assholes," he added under his breath before breaking into a small fit of coughing. "They ain't gettin' my money no more."

Themis found no communications at all on the manager's portable from the last 12 hours, except for a message from presumably the guy's wife lined with expletives complaining about some broken promise. Themis looked in the pack of cigarettes to find only cigarettes. Opening the manager's wallet though, Themis found ten one-unit AtlantiTrade notes, the same currency that he had just found in Trix's room, and that was on Trix's person. Themis took a picture for evidence.

"Where'd you get the cash?" Themis asked grimly.

"What, a guy can't carry around some money?" the manager retorted aggressively; he was not going to cooperate.

"You generally carry around 350 bucks worth of untraceable currency?"

"I generally carry around whatever the hell I want!" the manager indignantly spat back, his voice wheezing in the middle at the peak of his frustration.

Themis tucked his lips together, and shook his head in angry agreement. "Ok. Ok. I'm sure I'll be seeing you again soon," and he walked out.

"Yea screw you," the manager yelled after him raising his voice as he slammed his office door shut behind Themis.

Themis knew that he couldn't trace the cash since the bank encoded it for that very reason, but he did have cash that matched the note found in Trix's apartment, which pointed to a third party manipulating the situation. Themis headed back to the office to try to start figuring out how this all fit together, and to catch his next lead.

SEVEN

Barry was pacing his office. It was only mid afternoon, but he was on his fifth glass of scotch; it was only 3 days until the BER report came out, likely shattering his business. And even if it didn't kill his business, the fact that he blocked the search of Trix's apartment's surveillance footage was sure to come back to haunt him. The only thing at this point that could save Barry Arbitration was if Drake's plan was implemented, but the catalyst had failed, and with it Barry's problem lived: Molly.

Drake hadn't answered Barry's calls since the night Trix was shot, almost a week earlier. Barry kept trying to get through but Drake always had some excuse. Finally Barry decided to go down to Drake's office himself. After all, he had delivered on his end of the deal and Drake had fallen short. Barry figured that Drake was probably just embarrassed at his failure and busy revising the plan. He was sure that Drake was just waiting to get things in order before giving Barry an audience; at least he hoped that.

As Barry left his office, his secretary closed a window on her screen; she had been looking for a new job ever since BA issued the abnormal hold on the video footage from Trix's apartment building.

Barry took the level 1 pod to Drake's office building, finishing one more drink on the way. When he got there he had some artificial confidence flowing through his veins; after all, he thought again, he was in the right and Drake should be the one apologizing. Drake's secretary greeted Barry as if he had been given instructions on how to deal with this situation, just like the calls. The secretary was a dark-skinned young effeminate man with product in his black hair, and a stylish wrinkle-free suit. He wore a triangular badge with many different small stones, arranged by color in horizontal rows.

"I'm sorry, Mr. Barry, but you just missed Mr. Drake, can I leave a note for him?" The secretary said in a fake tone of disappointment.

"Oh I see," Barry sounded concerned, and was discouraged but not surprised. "I'll just make an appointment then," Barry said with a quick smile which his eyes betrayed as fake.

"How is Tuesday at 10?" the secretary asked politely, avoiding eye contact.

"No that's too late!" Barry blurted out, placing his hands on the secretary's desk making him visibly uncomfortable. "I mean, it's rather important. I, uh, would prefer to meet with him today," Barry finished, in a much calmer tone.

The secretary looked quickly but pointedly at Barry's hands on his desk, and could no longer hide the annoyance in his voice, "Well I'm sorry sir, but Mr. Drake is all booked through Monday." He stared at Barry with his eyebrows raised and lips tightly closed, hoping Barry would take the hint to leave.

Barry obviously got the hint but didn't care. "I see..." he said slowly with his hands still planted on the secretary's desk as his eyes darted to Drake's office door.

Drake's secretary likewise darted his gaze to Drake's door, frowning in anticipation of Barry's next move. His eyes were trained on Barry, burning into him, eyebrows still raised.

Barry shot towards the door, quickly shuffling in a jogging like motion which made him look like an awkward duck.

"Sir!" The secretary exclaimed in his deepest tone (which was not that deep), jumping to his feet.

"SIR!" He yelled as Barry's hand turned the knob. The secretary slammed a large button on the side of his desk which automatically deadbolted the office door, but it was too late as Barry had just managed to swing the door open before the bolt shot out, suspended horizontally from the side of the door.

The secretary came hustling behind Barry his face blushing, "Mr. Drake, sir, I'm sorry I tried to stop him but he just came right in – "

"It's okay, Benjamin, thank you, we're all right," Drake said dryly without much emotion. His secretary left like an obedient dog, slightly ashamed for having failed his master. "Have a seat Barry," and Drake motioned toward a chair, interlocking his fingers and placing his hands in front of him on his desk. He didn't speak, but just stared at Barry with his head tilted down condescendingly.

"Drake-" Barry said exasperated after a few moments of fidgeting in the chair, "why have you been ignoring me?"

Drake sighed and glanced to the side before meeting eyes with Barry again. Slowly he responded. "Barry... you know why I've been ignoring you, let's not play this game."

"But other agencies are going over my head! I'm ruined! Ted's release was frozen, and CCS got the warrant to search the cameras – which I tried to stop!" With this last statement Barry put his finger up, insisting he had done everything in his power to help the situation.

"Well that was stupid," Drake droned, bored.

"Stupid? STUPID?" Barry was in disbelief, raising his voice and sweating profusely, "Your Agents were on the recording! They would have been found out if I hadn't delayed the search! Have you forgotten that *I* delivered on my side of the bargain! It is *you* who owes *me!* Yet I continue to bend over backwards – "

Drake raised his voice but remained otherwise calm and almost droll. "It's over, Barry! I'm sorry, I truly am. But it's over, and you're finished. I'm not going down with you. I did all I could, but that druggie screwed up!" Drake shrugged. "That's just the way it goes this time!"

"Well..." Barry was starting to hyperventilate, searching for something to say, some course of action to take to right this. "Well I certainly won't release the evidence of AP's wrongdoing now!" Barry attempted a triumphant tone which failed.

Drake raised his palms up while shrugging again with a slight head tilt, and talked softer in a comforting tone, "No one would believe you if you did, Barry." When Barry didn't move Drake took out his mini-tab, "Tell you what," he transferred five thousand dollars onto a card which displayed the amount, and threw it down on the desk.

Barry looked at the money, his upper lip curled in disgust, and glared at Drake with greater disgust.

"Not enough?" Drake asked with fake sincerity.

"You might as well have dug my grave!" Barry growled, his dark tone showed he was accepting his fate, and realizing Drake was never his friend, despite his previous admiration for him.

"Now, Barry, you were screwed before I got involved... Just... well, maybe not quite *as* screwed."

Barry's stare seared into Drake's eyes while Drake looked back with the slightest of sympathy in his eyes, but strangely mixed with amusement. Barry shook his head, and stood up without taking the money on the desk. He took one more long look at Drake, nodding his head ever so slightly in cruel understanding with his jaw clenched. He turned around, and walked out of Drake's office silently, shutting the door calmly behind him. Drake's secretary looked at Barry with unsure eyes, not knowing what to expect, but Barry just walked tiredly out of the office without even noticing the secretary.

Stepping sullenly out of the NESA building Barry didn't notice the men in casual clothing watching him from across the street. "He's leaving Drake's building," one of the men said to his CCS partner, nudging him into action. The team sent updates directly to Themis, along with any pictures or video they took.

Back in his office, Drake pressed a couple of buttons on his telescreen and Agent White appeared. Without introduction, Drake said, "It didn't go so well with Barry. Let's clean this up."

"Yes sir." replied Agent White, and the call was ended.

Barry stumbled into his house that night around 22:00, considerably inebriated. It worked out for Drake's agents following him that he was drunk enough to leave the back door of his house, not just unlocked but, open. And perceiving the relative ease of this assignment, Agents White and Orange had let their guards down slightly, laughing about their target's intoxication, which worked out for the CCS Officers following Barry, and by extension the Agents.

Barry stumbled into his bar room, and managed to take a seat on one of the stools at the counter, almost falling off but stabilizing himself by grabbing hold of a beer tap. He let his success at arriving home and seating himself at the bar process, and let out a satisfied sigh as a drunken smile crossed his face. He was that level of wasted where even the impending doom of a shattered business and probable confinement seemed like minor obstacles, to be solved in the morning.

The bar room was dark and full of shadows, with just one bright buzzing light Barry had managed to switch on over the bar. It was an antique light up Crown Royal sign that Barry had bought years earlier – the company that made Crown Royal, of course, collapsed with the rest of the economy in the 2020's. The ceilings were high and the room was finished in stained mahogany. Barry reached across the bar and managed to grab a proper whiskey glass without breaking it; he snatched the bourbon whiskey on the second try – the first time only the top of the decanter came off in his hand, which amused Barry to the point where he burst into a light fit of drunken laughter.

The Agents sauntered into the barroom, their shadows waltzing slowly on the wall. Barry was mumbling to himself, having poured his whiskey with relative success, wetting the bar top a bit in the process. His gaze seemed to rest at about bar level, which could account for why he didn't notice the Agents in the mirror on the wall behind the bar. Standing in the doorway across the room, the Agents were surprised that after a minute Barry had still not noticed them.

Agent Orange shrugged at White with a smirk, grabbed a seat in one of the large maroon leather armchairs by the fireplace, leg crossed, and continued to watch Barry with an amused smile. After another 30 seconds or so, Agent White interrupted the mumbles.

"Hi Barry."

Suddenly the mumbling stopped, but it took Barry another few moments before he unsteadily swung around on the stool, and focused his eyes on the Agents with his head bobbing, and a hand on the bar for support. He gave a large hiccup which turned into a snort and chuckle.

"Gentlemen." Barry started quasi-politely, closing his eyes for a moment. Then opening his eyes, he continued with renewed energy, "Gentlemen! Of the esteemed – " he trailed off again. Another hiccup. "The *honorable...* Mr. Drake's employees... thugs... hitmen... true renaissance men!" Laughing, Barry raised his glass – sloshing a bit onto the floor – to the Agents, who wore amused smirks, and then slugged down about half of the oaky liquid. "Please –" hiccup "– please, help yourself to a drink fellas," Barry theatrically added, actually lighthearted, gesturing to the bar, and turned around back to face the bar, planting his elbows on the surface. Every so many blinks he would appear to momentarily doze off, just to open his eyes with a jerk of the body or a hiccup.

"Don't mind if I do," Agent Orange obliged as he fluidly stood up, and quickly crossed the room to the bar. He pulled a 16 ounce beer glass from under the bar, and filled it with the darker of the two beers on tap. He raised the glass to Barry, and with a crazy kind of smile and half closed eyes, Barry raised his glass as well. The two began to drink, and finished at the same time, pounding their glasses back to the bar triumphantly. Barry again started to chuckle, and Agent Orange joined him – laughing *at* Barry, not with him.

By this point Agent White had crossed the room and taken a seat next to Barry at the bar, observing the other two, amused. As Agent Orange laughed heartily – his straight white teeth on full display – he looked back and forth to White and Barry. White was smirking which showed his dimples, and shaking his head in mock disapproval. Orange raised the decanter toward Barry and cocked his head, nodded toward the whiskey, raising his eyebrows in a questioning manner.

"Hit me!" Barry said, his eyes barely open, and Agent Orange poured Barry a tall glass of whiskey, before filling his own beer glass a second time at the tap.

"So, Barry," Agent Orange began as he topped off his beer and pushed the tap back into place, foam crowning the glass with just one thin white drop trailing down the side, "Did you ever manufacture that evidence against Atlas?"

Barry started mumbling and got louder as he spat out, "Atlas!" then sunk back into unintelligible mumbles. "I was gnnn... gunn... release when thah bech mol murd durd."

The two Agents exchanged another amused glance.

With a chuckle, White quietly commented to his partner, "I hope you didn't get him *too* drunk."

Orange just shrugged with a smirk, as White turned to Barry and spoke.

"So that would be... on your safe drive?" he questioned.

Barry raised a finger as if he was going to make a point, but then put it down. He took another sip from his glass and again raised his finger. This time he stumbled to his feet and crossed the room to the doorway. Leaning on the door frame, he turned around to the Agents who hadn't moved, but were staring at Barry blankly. Barry gave them a rapid shaky beckoning wave with the hand that wasn't on the doorway supporting him. Understanding, the Agents quickly followed, Orange taking his beer with him.

In the kitchen, Barry put his finger against the DNA detector to allow a screen on the counter to light up and welcome him. "Izall ontheer" Barry stammered before collapsing into a kitchen chair still hiccuping every few seconds. White took his place at the screen and began typing and clicking. Orange stood in the doorway leaning against the trim, sipping his beer. A few minutes later White finished what he was doing, and wiped off the screen with a special cloth, before he clicked a button to make the screen recede back into the counter. Orange finished his beer, and licking his lips spoke to Barry who was nodding off at the table.

"Barry," Orange said loudly. "Barry!" this time, snapping his finger, he got his attention, and Mr. Barry looked up at Agent Orange like an obedient child. "Are you mad at Drake?" The agent asked loudly and clearly, a hint of baby talk in his words.

"I'm goig down." Barry said matter of factly with a shrug as he turned his gaze back to the table, "zall over, nufin lose." – shrug – "Drake down too?" – shrug – "Idunno- depends." Barry just kept shrugging, each time making the same ambivalent frown and repeating the last phrase, "Idunnodepends." He tried to raise a glass that wasn't there to his lips, only noticing when his hand touched his face, at which point he looked at his hand accusingly.

Agent Orange was looking at Barry and shaking his head in agreement, like a boss in the process of firing an employee.

"Come with me back to the bar," the Agent said as he turned in the doorway, and walked back toward the bar room. It took Barry a second to stumble to his feet, and Agent White walked up behind him to support him walking to the bar.

In the bar room Orange had put on a pair of black gloves, and taken a thin rope out of his pocket and was tossing one side over a sturdy light fixture in the center of the room. Agent Orange whistled a tune as he started tying one end of the rope in a loop. White led Barry back to his seat at the bar, and reunited him with his half empty glass of whiskey before taking the seat next to him once more. Barry huddled around his glass with both hands on it, elbows on the bar, head slumped looking into the glass. His hiccups were lighter and less frequent now, and he seemed to hardly even notice the agents' presence anymore.

Still whistling Agent Orange strolled across the room and began looping the other end of the rope to an ornate metal hook embedded deep into the hard wood mantel piece. Before tying the knot, Orange looked up at the light he hung the other end of the rope on, adjusting for length. Sauntering back over to the bar, Orange poured himself another half glass of beer, and immediately downed it. He rinsed out the glass, and wiped it with the same material White had used on the screen, also wiping down the outside and brim of the glass, and the beer tap. Agent White also pulled a pair of gloves out of his side pocket, and put them on.

Agent Orange walked back across the room, resuming his whistling, and dragged an armchair to the center of the room, as White dragged a bar stool, taller than the chair, to the center of the room next to it. White then walked to the bar and helped Barry to his feet.

"Wherwe go-n," Barry sputtered, eyes intermittently opening.

"Up the stairs to bed," White said softly, nurturing. "Here's a big step," he led Barry onto the chair, "And another big step" Barry was helped onto the stool, while Orange stood on his tip-toes to slip the noose around Barry's neck, and tighten it. White was still holding Barry's hand to stabilize him, "Now stand up straight, Mr. Barry." White used the same nurturing tone.

Barry had his hands out and his knees bent, shaking a bit, in an attempt to balance. Agent White stepped back, and Agent Orange kicked the top of the stool, which crashed to the floor at the same time Barry's neck snapped with a clear loud crack. The agents looked over the room once more to make sure they hadn't left any signs of their visit, and then left out the back door, the same way they came in.

As the Agents walked down the sidewalk away from Barry's house, the Corner Cop Security tail snapped some long off blurry pictures of the duo, and sent them over to Themis with a note about the two agents visiting Barry that night.

Back in the bar room one more shadow was added to the regular array. It swayed slowly on the wall, and on the bricks of the fireplace. Barry's body hanged, lifeless in the center of the room, with the Crown Royal sign over the bar offering the only flickering light.

The main story the next morning was the evidence release from Barry Arbitration which supposedly pointed to Atlas Protection as tampering with evidence in order to nail Ted Lanta for the murder, and thus avoid the destruction of the Lanta distillery business when Ted took over. Atlas Protection had managed to survive the first wave of angry customers and dropped policies when Barry first announced the reversal of Ted's indictment, but this was even worse. Customers didn't want to hear that they had to wait another month for the independent assessment of the evidence to see who was really at fault.

Usually the office would be like a ghost town on a Saturday, but Atlas Protection was in full damage control mode. Atlas was forced to offer all sorts of incentives just to keep his customers, and AP was running low on operating cash, having waived thousands of fees for customers until this was all settled. With all the news out, banks were not interested in taking a risk to loan AP money. Mr. Atlas wondered if he would be able to keep the company afloat until the final review came out.

He decided to give Molly a call to ask if BER could release some details that would at least cast doubt on Barry Arbitration's legitimacy. Molly agreed to give an interview to preview the BER report on Barry Arbitration that was scheduled for release on Monday. Mr. Atlas was watching as the interview came on a popular news feed.

"Frankly, we want to urge all customers to wait for the independent review before deciding whether to keep Atlas Protection or drop their policies," Molly explained. "Even BER's report scheduled for release the day after tomorrow will give some signals that this scandal may not be all it is chalked up to be. At this time, I can confirm that Mr. Barry of Barry Arbitration took a personal bribe to transfer one of BA's cases to another arbitration agency. Because of this action, and others, BA will be downgraded by Business Ethics Review. While BER has no direct knowledge of the case of Atlas Protection, we would advise skepticism of anything to come out of Barry Arbitration."

The station cut back to a reporter, "That statement coming from Molly Metis of Business Ethics Review regarding Barry Arbitration, the morning after the evidence against Atlas Protection was made public. Mr. Reed Barry has not been reached for comment, and could not be seen entering his office, or leaving his home this morning. Repeated attempts to call and knock on his door have not – hold on I am getting some updated information as this story unravels.

"I am being told that a female friend of Mr. Barry's entered his home this morning, and inside, found Mr. Barry hanged, in an apparent suicide, with a suicide note written on his counter tablet. He was pronounced dead at the scene. Further details to come as this story takes a dark twist. Indeed customers may want to withhold judgment of Atlas Protection until all the details are sorted out.

"In other news, Transcend Space Travel has announced a breakthrough technology that will allow customers five day travel between Earth and Mars. Stocks surged nearly 2,000% after the initial announcement..."

Mr. Atlas stared at the screen with his jaw agape. Feeling a twinge of guilt, Atlas realized he was happy that Barry had killed himself, because this made the evidence release fade in comparison. Now the focus would be on what made Barry kill himself, rather than on the evidence – fake as it may be – against Atlas Protection. Atlas instructed his employees to bring up the suicide, but try to remain civil, in an attempt to deter customers from dropping their policies. The independent review could not come soon enough.

Eating breakfast, Officer Themis had been watching the same interview as Atlas. As he learned of Barry's "suicide" he nearly spit his coffee across the room. On big cases, Themis turned into a bit of a workaholic, and had already seen the pictures of the two agents leaving Barry's house the night before. But CCS was the only agency with that information at this time, and there was no other reason to suspect that his death was not a suicide.

"I've gotta get to the office!" Themis burst out to his family as he quickly pushed his seat out and grabbed his jacket and portable.

"What's wrong?" his wife asked, concerned.

"I don't think that was a suicide, and I have pictures of who's behind it. This is big honey, I'll call you. No idea when I'll be home. Love you." He kissed his wife and kids, and ran out the door, leaving Mrs. Themis bewildered in the kitchen.

Themis grabbed a pod to go see Drake and question him about Barry's visit to his office the evening before.

In the lobby of Drake's office, Drake's secretary eyed Officer Themis suspiciously, recognizing Themis's badge as a security badge, and asked in a testy tone, "Can I help you?"

"I need to speak to Mr. Drake about a security matter."

Flustered, the secretary looked at Drake's schedule and back at Themis. "Do you have an appointment?"

"No I don't but this is an important matter, Mr. Drake's cooperation will make this a lot easier."

Sensing that Drake would want to avoid such an interview, the secretary began to make up an excuse about why Drake was not in his office, when Drake popped his head out.

"Benjamin I need you to get ahold of Mr. Patrick and-" Drake began to order calmly before looking up, mildly startled to see an Officer in his lobby.

"Oh you *are* in," Officer Themis said sarcastically, smirking and casting a sharp glance toward Drake's secretary, who blushed despite his dark complexion, and just stared at his computer screen.

"My name is Officer Themis," he said walking over to Drake and extending his hand.

Drake was obviously caught off guard; he shook Themis's hand silently, before stammering his own introduction, "Ah yes, I'm Mr. Drake. Won't you join me in my office?"

Drake closed the door and took a seat behind his desk, flashing a short slightly detectable smile toward Themis to be polite. Drake then folded his hands on his desk, and stared at Themis waiting for his explanation.

It was a few awkward moments before Officer Themis spoke, he was trying to get a feel for Drake.

"Beautiful office," Themis said cheerfully to Drake, with a smile.

Drake just raised his eyebrows for a moment and remained silent, still staring at Themis. Themis cleared his throat and dropped the smile. "I wanted to ask you a couple of questions about Mr. Barry."

Though his heart skipped, Mr. Drake's appearance did not change in the slightest. His usual calm and collected poker face was an asset in situations like these. A few seconds passed before Drake spoke.

"Mr. Barry was a friend of mine. NESA is also a customer of BA, though we will be switching our main representation this week, for obvious reasons. I was disturbed to hear about his suicide." Drake spoke low and without emotion.

"Could you see any indication of why Barry would commit suicide?" Officer Themis asked.

"Well, the news reports can give us some insight there. It seems Mr. Barry was involved in some less than ethical business practices. I think he saw the writing on the wall, and knew his business would be ruined. Obviously NESA would not have continued to do business with BA under the circumstances, despite Barry being a friend of mine."

"Could you tell he was depressed, especially over the past few days?"

"I haven't seen much of Barry over the past week or so. I think he crawled inside a bottle when he knew he couldn't outrun these problems," Drake drawled.

"But specifically when you saw Mr. Barry yesterday at 15:25. Was there any indication that Mr. Barry would end his own life?"

Drake sat silently, staring down Officer Themis, the periphery of the office losing focus as his sight narrowed, and his gaze turned more acidic by the second. How did Officer Themis know that Barry had visited his office the day before, and what else did he know? Could he have connected Drake to Barry's death? Drake's heart was racing, but he wouldn't let that show.

"There was no indication," Drake replied deep and slow.

"None? What exactly did Barry come to see you about yesterday anyway?"

Another pause. "Officer... Themis is it? I'm afraid I won't be able to answer any further questions without a personal arbiter present."

Officer Themis didn't move, but stared at Drake unflinching. "Okay." Themis eventually said, with a hint of suspicion in his voice. Themis couldn't help but ask one more question, just to see if anything about Drake's stony demeanor changed.

"Just one more question," Themis said as he walked toward the door, turning back to Drake, "through your business dealings, or your personal relationship with Mr. Barry... is there anyone who would want him dead?"

Drake began to speak but his voice cut out, forcing him to clear his throat. "hem, It's easy to make enemies in this business...."

Themis gave a final nod before leaving the office, "Thanks for your time."

Drake was worried. If Themis knew that Barry had come to see him the afternoon before, he may also know the Agents visited Barry's home. It wouldn't be easy, but it would be possible for the dots to be connected if the Agents were identified – although they had taken pains to be unidentifiable, in order to excel in their field of work.

Drake knew he needed to contain this, but he couldn't initiate his ultimate plan without something solid to blame on drug cartels from outside of New England. The attempted murder of Molly had been attributed to outside drugs, thanks in part to Drake's control of the popular news outlet, News of New England, but it was generally viewed as an isolated incident. He had originally thought that a string of murders would be best, but there was no time to plan for that. He needed one big, brutal event, linked to the home invasion of Molly.

Drake figured he could also have stories on queue in case it was revealed that Barry had actually been murdered. He would give the impression that drug cartel activity was heating up in the region, and that fragmented security companies couldn't handle the influx of unsavory characters. Molly's home invasion would be framed as an attempt to silence the media about the rising concerns of drug cartels, thus far successful. Barry's murder would be cast as a hit to prevent prosecution of a high-level cartel leader. And what better fit than if the head investigator for Corner Cop Security, handling Molly's case and involved in Barry's case, was brutally murdered in his home along with his adorable family?

Drake would put out the story that drug cartel hitmen were streaming into New England from New York to further disrupt the system, within a short period of time, and establish their control over an unsuspecting area, that was insufficiently prepared for this type of turmoil. The stories from News of New

England would be enough to fuel the rumor for long enough that Drake could "save the day" with NESA intervening.

This time Drake wouldn't make the mistake of having an unreliable drug addict perform the task. He would have Agent White and Agent Orange take care of Themis. If he planned the murder for the following night, that would give him enough time to get the news stories ready for release at strategic times. The following morning after the attack, the border would be initiated, when Themis's body was discovered and known drug cartel members were stopped from entering New England.

Drake was nervous, but he thought he could pull it off. Anyway, he didn't have much time to waste, it could be any day that the right pieces would be put together. Without Themis there would be no one to sound the alarm about Drake's connection to Barry and Molly. Drake had to pull this all together before it started unraveling.

EIGHT

The next day Molly invited Mr. Atlas out to dinner, and he was happy to oblige. His spirits had been lifted by the shift from his supposed wrongdoing, to the story about Barry's unsavory business ethics and suicide. Molly was working on her next piece, connecting the dots of the events unfolding. Mr. Atlas was part of the story, but Molly also respected his insight and opinions. She was talking through what she had so far.

"I think that the break-in at my house is somehow connected. It doesn't make sense that the electronics would have been the focus, or that he would try to –" Molly took a deep breath, but tried to downplay it, "– um, kill me," she tried to remove emotion and focus on the facts. "And the only big story I was working on at the time was about Barry Arbitration. And BA made up the story and manufactured the evidence against Atlas protection – we just need to wait for the independent review for confirmation."

Atlas was shaking his head in agreement, "It is just unfortunate for me that those reviews take so long. Though to be fair, they are doing the investigation the right way so it is hard to complain."

"Have things gotten any better since yesterday morning?" Molly asked.

"Well, the deluge of cancellations has slowed, yes. But it is going to take months – possibly a year – to undo the damage caused, after the independent review. I've filed for damages against BA for once the review finds that the evidence was fake. But I suspect there may be a lot of people seeking restitution from BA. Their insurance kicked in this morning to place all their customers with other arbiters. It's just a matter of dismantling NESA now, who gets what."

"The piece I don't understand is why BA would have it out for AP. You guys aren't even competitors so it can't be something as simple as that. Can you think of any reason why Barry would want to damage you or your business?"

Atlas paused, thinking. "Nothing stands out. I mean we have had our small differences in the past, but what arbiter and security company haven't? All I can think of is that Barry was paid off to hurt my business, since we are a blooming company. And we do know now that Barry was open to that sort of bribery." Atlas didn't mind the business side of this dinner, but was enjoying the social side more. Every time he found himself with Molly his spirits were lifted.

Molly was taking notes and thinking hard, "Remember when this whole thing started with BA holding that news conference? News of New England started talking about the tiny amount of stock you own in Illicit Liquors. Do you have any history with NNE?"

Again Atlas thought, looking up and to the left. He slowly started shaking his head, "No... but now that I think about it, they have taken shots at me before. When we announced that we were beginning to form street divisions they ran a whole segment questioning if we had the expertise, blah blah blah. They kept contrasting us with NESA, saying that since New England Security Agency started as a street team, they had the foundation and knew how to do the job better. It was stupid, I don't think anyone really picked up on it."

Molly grabbed her tablet off the table and started typing while she asked curiously, "Is NESA your main competitor for street teams?"

Atlas loved watching Molly work. *She is so resilient*, he thought.

"Yea, and they do a pretty good job. I guess that's why they were being held as the standard by NNE," Atlas hadn't given it much thought.

"Maybe not." Molly said without looking up from her screen.

"What's that?"

"Guess who owns 55% of News of New England?"

"Oh, I don't know," Atlas said pondering, distracted, "I always thought it had a broad stockholder base."

"Mr. Drake of New England Security Agency owns a controlling stake – 55% – of the popular news site News of New England," Molly read off her tablet screen.

Atlas was looking suspiciously – not at Molly but over the implications for NESA. "You don't think..."

Molly interrupted and continued reading, "The company gained a stellar reputation among consumers in 2056 for its unyielding opposition to Unified New America, the quasi-American-government which sought to impose monopoly force over the people of New England...blah blah blah... Despite NESA running into some minor setbacks after switching to Barry Arbitration in 2109, the company has remained profitable since its inception during the New England Renaissance of the 2040's."

Molly looked up at Atlas, wearing a most serious look on her face. Atlas's face likewise betrayed his concern, but he would not let emotion get the best of him.

"Let's not jump to conclusions here..." He sounded like he was trying to convince himself.

"I think we should go talk to Officer Themis, he's the head CCS investigator handling my case."

They paid their bill and took a pod to Themis's neighborhood. Molly messaged Themis on the way over to let him know they were coming. When the two arrived, Atlas introduced himself, and the three settled down at Themis's kitchen table. It was getting late. Mrs. Themis came over and introduced herself; she understood how important this case was.

"Can I get you three anything? Some coffee, dessert?"

"I could go for a cup of coffee, thanks," Atlas said with a smile.

"Me as well, if you don't mind," Molly added, also with a friendly smile.

"Sounds like coffee all around," Themis agreed, giving his wife a nod, "Thanks honey."

Turning his focus to Molly and Atlas, Themis asked warmly, "So what was it you wanted to speak with me about tonight, Molly?"

"Well, I was discussing the latest article I am working on with Mr. Atlas. We were trying to figure out why BA would target his company. We don't have anything solid, but what we did find out is that NESA was a customer of Barry Arbitration, and that Drake owns NESA *and* a controlling stake in NNE. News of New England figures in because they seeded the story about Atlas's stake in Illicit Liquors, even though it's only $5000 worth of stock."

Themis was taking it all in and shaking his head in agreement. "Can I speak off the record?" Themis asked Molly.

"Of course," Molly quickly responded, "This is all off the record."

"Drake has come under some suspicion. It seems Barry went to see Drake two evenings ago, just hours before Barry committed suicide. Two unidentified men were also seen entering and leaving Barry's house around the time of the suicide, but that has been kept out of the media for now. There was nothing else to suggest foul play, no fingerprints, DNA, broken windows, etcetera."

Molly's eyebrows were raised, and Atlas wore a shocked look as well. "This is too much to be a coincidence," Molly said looking between the two men.

Atlas looked like he was trying to put it all together. "So are we saying that Drake and Barry had something going on? Could they both have been threatened by the same people?"

"But that still wouldn't explain why you were attacked by News of New England, and why I was targeted by someone," Molly added.

"If the third party needed to manipulate both Barry Arbitration and New England Security Agency..." Themis was thinking out loud, slowly articulating his ponderings, "in order to target each of you... but that still wouldn't explain *why* they were targeting you."

"Officer Themis," Molly started.

"Please, call me James."

"Okay. James. Do you have any idea who the men were that left Barry's house on the night of his suicide?"

"We don't know... the pictures were too obscured for facial recognition. It's possible some technology tampered with the signal, or it just happened to be a blurry picture set. But obviously, that would answer a lot of questions."

"It sounds like they are advanced," Atlas chimed in. "If they have the technology to jam a signal like that."

"Well I don't know for sure, like I said, it could have just been a bad shot. They *were* dressed pretty well, though."

"What if," Molly began looking off somewhere, "Barry was coerced by someone who thought he would squeal when my report came out on BA?"

Mrs. Themis put coffee down in front of each of them.

"I'm heading off to bed, don't you three work too hard," Mrs. Themis joked with a sweet smile, and left the room after kissing her husband on the cheek.

"So what you're saying, Molly," Atlas returned them to the subject at hand, "Is that Barry could have been coerced to frame me, and whoever coerced him didn't think they could trust him to keep quiet?"

Officer Themis gave it some thought. "That would account for why Molly's electronics were stolen. Whoever it is, didn't want the report on Barry to come out, because then some stones were going to be unturned, and maybe someone would look into who threatened Barry. It makes sense, too, that they used Trix to attack Molly, since he would be easily bribed or threatened."

"I don't know..." Atlas skeptically interjected. "Did Barry seek out Drake to protect him then? Or was Drake coerced as well? After all, it was Drake's News of New England which made such a big deal out of my holdings of Illicit Liquors."

"Is that it?" Molly asked. "Was it the owners of Illicit Liquors the whole time, trying to keep Teddy out of jail? So they make it look like Atlas framed Ted, and threatened Barry to support that claim with his arbitration agency. And then what, threatened Drake to support that story with News of New England?" She finished shaking her head, thinking it sounded a bit far fetched.

Themis had both palms on his coffee mug and was looking attentively between Molly and Atlas. "They could have chosen Barry knowing he was sketchy, but not knowing a BER report was in the works. When they found *that* out, they needed to get rid of the report, or else their coercion of Barry would be revealed."

There was a pause as the three considered this scenario.

"I'm skeptical," Atlas added. "Why Drake? There are plenty of news agencies that could have seeded the story."

"Not big ones with singular control." Molly retorted. "There are small news sites with single owners, and large ones with a bunch of owners. News of New England is unique in that it is large, and has a majority holding by a single person: Drake."

"There was something odd about Drake when I interviewed him." Themis said. "He *could* have been scared... but really? I mean the CEO of the biggest security agency in New England being threatened by a company without direct access to agents and gunmen?"

"That's what's not making sense. If I know Drake, anyone threatening him would have another thing coming," Atlas added this insight on his competitor.

"Unless it wasn't a threat of violence." Molly almost asked. "Maybe Drake and Barry were in with some sketchy dealings, and Ted's family blackmailed them. That explains all the AtlantiTrade notes floating around."

Agent White and Agent Orange pulled up outside of Themis's house in a beat up white four door sedan. NESA had confiscated the vehicle during an arrest of a known cartel member for an assault against an NESA customer when they were visiting New York. But those records had been doctored, and the car was all set to be connected to the drug cartel the next morning – the smoking gun.

The agents were not dressed in their usual suits, but instead looked like stereotypical drug dealers, but with an upper-class touch that only real druggies would detect. Hooded sweatshirts and jeans with some popular combat style boots worn mostly by thugs and posers these days. They still wore their sunglasses, which they linked together so that each could tap into the others' video feed. The Agents sat waiting to get the go ahead from Drake.

"Oh my God!" Themis exclaimed. "I saw two guys outside of Trix's adap the day after you were attacked Molly. I completely forgot; they could be the same guys that left Barry's. They certainly dressed the same."

"So then the only missing piece is why Drake would go along with Ted's family," Atlas concluded.

Molly still looked skeptical.

"You don't buy it?" asked Themis.

"No it's not that... I just feel like there is still another missing piece. We need to know who those agents are if we really want to find out who they are working for, now that they are connected to two crime scenes."

A car door shut outside.

"That's weird," said Themis, "There are only a couple people with cars in this neighborhood, strange that they would be driving so late." He stood up to look out the window and saw two thugs walking briskly toward his door, guns drawn. "Get upstairs, go, NOW!" Themis yelled to his confused guests.

The two stood up and started toward the stairs, "What's going on?" Molly asked, concerned as Themis herded them to the second floor.

Just then the side door of the house could be heard slamming open with an enormous crash, and Mrs. Themis rushed into the upstairs hallway as Officer Themis pushed past her into their bedroom to get his gun.

"What's going on?" a tired and scared Mrs. Themis croaked in confusion.

"Grab the kids and lock the bedroom door; Molly, Mr. Atlas, go into the bedroom with her."

Themis guarded the hallway as his wife, the two kids, barely awake, and Molly rushed into the master bedroom and looked out, waiting for Atlas. But Mr. Atlas had pulled out his own small black handgun that looked like something a secret agent would carry.

"I'm not letting you go down there alone," he said calmly to Themis.

Officer Themis considered his options, but silently nodded, thankful for the help. The bedroom door was shut, and Themis quietly peered around the corner down the stairs. He could hear slow footsteps that sounded like they were in the kitchen, or possibly the living room. There were hushed voices speaking to each other, but he couldn't make out what they were saying.

"Themis," Atlas whispered, his mini-tab in one hand, semi-auto in the other, "I'm offline. I can't call for help."

Themis motioned for the two to switch positions. Themis pulled out his own tablet, and hit the emergency button. Nothing. He had Internet access, but a pang of interference kept blocking the connection, and offering up signal noise instead.

"They're using some sort of jammer," Themis whispered to Atlas as he took his spot back at the top of the stairs, "I don't think these are druggies."

A black combat boot appeared around the doorway at the bottom of the stairs, and a dark figure could be seen slowly rounding the corner. Themis aimed, slowly exhaled, and gingerly pulled on the trigger. BAM! The second shot was not as well placed. BAM!

The first bullet struck the figure at the bottom of the stairs dead center, and he tumbled backwards out of view, yelling loudly, "Son of a bitch!"

The second shot went into the front wall of the house. Themis didn't move. He waited. He could hear loud moans and shuffling in the living room. Then he heard the sound of poly-melding-elastomer being pulled apart, and another loud exclamation in the same voice, "God-Damn-it!"

"Did he have a vest?" asked Atlas surprised and hushed.

"I think so... pretty well-equipped thugs," Themis added sarcastically.

There were more whispers downstairs back and forth, but not quite as hushed as before. It sounded like a slight argument ensued, and the voice of the man who had been shot was finally heard angrily saying, "No, I'll do it." There was silence; one pair of footsteps faded, and then the sound of whatever was left of the kitchen door being shut. Atlas and Themis exchanged questioning glances.

Suddenly a gunshot was heard from downstairs in the living room, accompanied by something metal being hit. Then the same thing in the kitchen and then the dining room, spaced moments apart.

Next there was the sound of smashing glass. Thin glass, not a window, a cabinet. Listening attentively, Themis glanced side to side, thinking about why this thug would be breaking into his liquor cabinet. This didn't seem like the time to dull the pain from the stopped bullet. But he wasn't drinking the alcohol, he was pouring it. Multiple bottles of hard liquor sloshed out, spread around the living room, dining room, and kitchen. Then a full glass bottle of vodka came slamming hard halfway up the stairs from around the corner, and shattered with vodka dripping slowly down the steps.

Themis realized what was happening. He turned to Atlas "Go tell the others to stay put as long as possible, one of these guys is still waiting outside. Open the window but be careful." Atlas turned to follow his orders.

The swooshing sounds of a large fire being suddenly lit in the living room could be heard from the upstairs hallway, and an orange glow grew on the downstairs wall. Themis waited, his heart pounding, trying to decide the best course of action. He didn't hear the other thug leave; one was in the house, one was waiting outside.

The crackling fire could be heard from the living room. Smoke was starting to make its way up the stairs, and the fire was casting growing and flickering light further up the staircase. Themis had to act before the fire reached the stairs and he was trapped. It occurred to him that the gunshots moments earlier were the thug shooting the fire detectors for the sprinkler system.

Since the fire was large and growing in the living room, Themis figured the thug must have been waiting for him in the dining room, to the left at the bottom of the stairs. Slowly he crept down the stairs, removing his shoes as to muffle the sounds of his steps. The smoke was quickly becoming unbearable as the column rising up the stairs thickened, getting blacker by the second.

At the bottom of the stairs, Themis paused with his back against the wall, slightly crouched with both hands on his 9mm. He wanted to take a deep breath, but was afraid the smoke would make him cough and give away his position. Luckily, Themis heard a muffled cough come from the dining room, giving him an idea of where the thug laid in wait.

Acting quickly before the thug had a chance to reposition himself, Themis dove from his position on the second and third stairs, rolling onto the floor between the dining room and living room and quickly popping up and aiming in a kneeling position with one foot planted on the ground in front of him.

The thug got a shot off first, but it buzzed past Themis – he swore he felt the wind from it – and shattered a window in the living room. Smoke began to pour outside. Themis was quick to return fire though, his training kicking in like Pavlov's dogs. He squeezed off two shots before the thug got his second shot off – that one went into the ceiling as the thug collapsed and crumpled to the ground. Themis' first bullet had gone directly into the center of the thug's forehead, exiting the back with some blood and bits of brain, forming a flying saucer shape on the light yellow wall, darkening as the smoke stained it.

As Themis ran to the kitchen in combat position he kept his gun trained on the lifeless body, until he was sure the man was down for good.

The sprinkler in the kitchen was working despite the bullet lodged in the sensor. Already a layer of water covered the floor, as a thick spray continued to rain down, soaking Themis in the few seconds it took him to run through the kitchen. He paused for a moment at the door as he had done on the stairs. Then he burst outside quickly glancing to his right before jumping into a prone position on the porch, aiming down the side of his house toward the back where the second thug knelt aiming up at the open bedroom window. The window was open and bullet holes had chewed off pieces of the window frame. The thug turned toward Themis and fired, the bullets digging into the porch planks and railings, splinters randomly bursting loose like little wooden geysers. From the upstairs window two shots rained down on the thug who was crouched and slowly retreating backwards, narrowly missing, or perhaps grazing his sweatshirt. He turned and returned fire to the window, and Themis heard Atlas yell out in pain. Themis lifted himself up a bit and fired rapidly at the thug, who fired once more back toward Themis before fleeing through the back neighbor's yard.

Themis pursued him far enough to make sure he wasn't coming back, then quickly returned to his house, the front of the first floor increasingly engulfed in flames. Mrs. Themis had already torn open the window sill to access the rope ladder embedded in the wall for emergency escape. The older boy was halfway down, and his younger sister was beginning the descent. Themis grabbed his son by the waist and brought him safely to the ground, then coaxed his younger daughter down with encouraging words. Molly was next, and quickly embraced the kids to comfort them once Themis helped her down.

Mrs. Themis poked her head out of the window and yelled down, "Atlas got hit in the arm, I'm going to send him down but he needs your help!"

As Atlas swung his legs out of the window, an emergency response skyship floated into range outside, having been called by the neighbors who saw the fire and heard the gunshots.

Four men repelled from the low hovering ship and rushed toward the injured as a hose extended from the skyship and began spraying flame retardant foam on the roof.

Knowing he wouldn't get another opportunity, Themis ran toward the kitchen door, covered his mouth with his shirt, and ignoring the protesting yells from the emergency response team, barreled back inside, this time armed with his mini-tab.

The kitchen sprinklers had stopped, and the blaze had worked its way to the doorway between the kitchen and the living room. The smoke was thick, so Themis dropped to his knees and sloshed through the kitchen still an inch deep in water, into the dining room, where flames were quickly approaching the thug's body, already searing his left foot.

Themis' shirt slipped and he breathed in a mouthful of thick smoke, initiating a coughing fit that didn't stop even as he fixed his shirt's position. Working quickly Themis snapped a picture of the thugs face, pocketed his sunglasses, grabbed the corpse's thick head of hair, and jerked it closer for a better angle, then snapped another picture. Still coughing, Themis crawled on his forearms as fast as possible back toward the kitchen door as something heavy crashed down in the living room amongst the crackling flames and black smoke that now engulfed the entire house.

Themis stood up, bursting through the kitchen door into the arms of two waiting rescuers, who quickly ushered him away from the house, and sat him down on the sidewalk while his coughing fit persisted. The rescue skyship was working its way down the house, quelling the largest flames first. As a second medical transport skyship arrived and landed gracefully on the street, an emergency SUV screeched to a halt on the scene. The skyship door opened and medical personnel stormed out.

An EMT ran over with an oxygen mask as Themis' family tearfully crowded around him, his wife scolding him for reentering the burning home.

Atlas was already on a stretcher, sitting up, with an EMT bandaging his arm. He gave Themis a reassuring nod as they met eyes.

"You went back for a picture didn't you?" Molly asked Themis, standing back a few feet from the family, arms crossed as she shivered, hair messy across her face. She was still in a bit of shock, especially with this being the second attack she had survived in as many weeks.

Themis took out his mini-tab and removed his oxygen mask. His voice was hoarse; "Thanks for reminding me, I need to send these into the office for facial recognition. Maybe that will tell us how Drake's involved in all this. Those weren't hired druggies in there, like Trix." Themis looked at his screen to send the photos.

Themis's wife chimed in, "I want you to go to the hospital before doing any more work! And do you mind filling me in on why our house got burnt down and we got shot at on the way out?" Her tone was understandably frantic with a note of sarcasm, suggesting she couldn't quite make light of the situation, but understood that certain things took precedent in a crisis.

"Hold on, before we go," Themis got to his feet and beckoned over the detective who had arrived in the SUV to start the investigation and take witness statements. Themis knew him, since CCS plans were included in his pay. "Jackson, I need you to have someone bring these sunglasses down to the office and give them to the team that's looking at the pictures I just sent in. I'll be in as soon as I can, this is all linked with Barry, and the break-in at Molly's."

"Ok, make sure you're ok. But I'm sending someone with you to the hospital to take your statement before you forget anything. Let me know as soon as you're in and we'll talk everything out."

Themis gave Jackson a nod, and replaced his mask as a nurse led Themis and his family toward the rescue skyship. Atlas was already on board, and Molly joined by his side, holding onto the arm that had not suffered a gunshot wound, as the skyship lifted off toward the hospital.

Agent White was running down the sidewalk of a street a couple blocks away from Themis's house. As the police data streamed across his glasses, White would take a left, or a right, or cut through a yard to avoid being caught. He was out of breath, and bleeding from his left arm which had been grazed by a bullet – though he hadn't even noticed yet.

Agent White was finally a safe distance away, and the sirens were only a faded distant sound. Skyships had been deployed to search for the fleeing arsonist, so White grabbed a pod, and entered a busy location with plenty of bars that would still be open at this hour. He needed to make sure his steps wouldn't be traced.

Inside the pod, Agent White looked at his arm noticing the gunshot wound, but decided that he could wait to patch it up – his dark sweatshirt wouldn't show much blood. Then he took a deep breath, and made a call to Drake.

Drake was not sleeping, he was at home anxiously awaiting the phone call from his agents, with news releases ready to go, and orders waiting to be issued. He saw White's call coming in through his desk screen, and answered.

"Is it done?" he said quickly without expression.

"Themis is still alive, Orange is dead. The house burnt down, you should be able to see it on the news already. Our car is still there, they might have already made the connection to the cartel."

Drake said nothing, just stared silently at the blank screen with White's voice coming through it. He didn't know what he felt; some mixture of anger and fear, with a little sadness thrown in, but overpowered by rage. "Okay," He finally let out quickly, shaking his head in agreement, "Okay." he repeated. "I'll be in contact," and he shut off the screen. Drake bit his thumbnail, a nervous habit when he was thinking.

He waited for a moment, still. He hadn't gotten rid of Themis, which was a problem, but at least the attack had been big and noticeable. Drake could not suppress his disappointment that Agent Orange had been killed, since he relied on the team of Agents for his most important and unsavory assignments. But he couldn't dwell on it now. This was crisis time and he couldn't let it go to waste – it was time to exploit the problem he had created so that NESA could "solve" it.

Back in the pod when the transmission cut out, Agent White swore loudly and kicked angrily at anything in reach, shattering the plastic cover on the front of the pod's wall. He put his head in his hand thinking about his dead partner, his throbbing arm, and his failed mission. He tried to calm himself as he got out of the pod at his destination. He walked down the street until he found the busiest watering hole, and posted up at the bar with a strong drink. It would be hours before they could trace his movement to the area, and anyway they still wouldn't be able to identify him by his face, his glasses still intact. White had severed communication between his and Agent Orange's glasses when he saw Themis's face hovering over Agent Orange's body in the smoky room, taking pictures.

Drake had arrived at his office, and flipped through a couple of channels until he found the story he was looking for. He kept two telescreens in his office in order to monitor more news feeds at once. There were so many different websites for news, each with their own live streaming channel, that Drake would have the two telescreens cycle through some preset channels finding important stories. A young female reporter stood outside of the smoking remains of Themis's house, emergency lights flashing all around her on the still dark residential street.

"A vicious attack at the home of Officer James Themis has left two men hospitalized, and one suspect dead; another, on the run. The home of Officer Themis, the lead investigator for Corner Cop Security, was broken into after 23:00 last night, as the officer entertained two guests, one of whom, Molly Metis, a reporter for Business Ethics Review, was herself a recent victim of a violent home invasion. Ironically the other guest is the president of a major security company, Kittery Atlas of Atlas Protection."

This was news to Drake, and though a pang of worry at first gripped him, he quickly decided this would benefit him, only helping the public to connect the two attacks.

"There is some speculation on whether the two attacks are connected;" the broadcast continued, "a car owned by a known drug cartel member from New York was found outside Themis's home, while the surviving suspect fled on foot. Reports suggest the suspect who was shot and killed after breaking into Molly Metis' home last week was also a member of the same drug cartel, leading many to conclude that both Metis and Themis, head violent crimes investigator for Corner Cop Security, were targeted systematically by the same, deadly cartel. That Kitt Atlas was a third high-profile victim only fans the flames of speculation."

Perfect, Drake thought, they already picked up the first bit of misinformation put out there by NNE without fact checking, in an attempt to give a quick, gripping story to the public.

"Themis and Atlas were admitted into an area hospital with non-life-threatening injuries; the rest of the family escaped without any major physical harm."

Drake was feeling good about the setup, and he sent a message to a trusted NNE reporter who had another story waiting for release. Refreshing the home page, Drake saw the story appear with a bold red headline after the uppercase phrase: "BREAKING NEWS."

The story started by recounting the events of just hours earlier, and naming the drug cartel involved. Then it became the first outlet to report that Mr. Barry was in fact murdered, mixing truth with fiction by reporting that Barry was murdered by the same thugs who broke into Themis's home and set it on fire. The article explained that Barry Arbitration had been secretly investigating the Cartel, and preparing multiple warrants for a crackdown targeting suspects from a variety of unsolved New England crimes, as the cartel expanded its New England influence. CCS was to execute the warrants this very morning, the article continued, which sparked the late night attack on CCS' head investigator, Themis. Molly had been attacked earlier in a successful attempt to keep the story out of the headlines. The article urged people to remain indoors for at least 24 hours, since undisclosed sources claimed more attacks were coming, possibly on a larger scale.

By the time the sun started to rise over the Atlantic, the News of New England article had been picked up by most area news outlets, and repeated relentlessly. Drake prepared a statement as his customers clamored for more details, and reassurances that they would be safe. But first he sent word to his men, and Mr. Patrick sent word to his, that all traffic coming into New England was to be halted at the border, and rerouted to stations under NESA or Minutemen Arms control. Every officer was called in on emergency, and by the time most people in the "border" towns awoke, patrols of heavily armed police battalions were marching through their streets.

Drake gazed out his arched office window as the first rays of light shone through. His employees were already mustering, and the cameras were ready. Drake sat down at his desk with the cameras rolling to make a statement.

He was calm, as always, and spoke slowly and deeply. Confidence bristled from every pore of Drake's body.

"People of New England, we are in a crisis. As you have undoubtedly heard, a drug cartel from New York has implemented a series of attacks against the media, arbiters, and security officers. As the largest security company in New England, it is my duty, not only to the customers of New England Security Agency, but to every honest inhabitant of New England, to keep you and your family safe.

"NESA cares about more than just profits, we care about the future of peace and stability in our beloved region. Many of you remember the interim years before order was restored, and I vow to each and every one of you that under my watch, chaos will never return to New England! That is why, effective immediately and until further notice, NESA and our partners will secure every home, business, street, and person in New England against all crimes.

"In the interest of security, today in New England we cannot rely on fragmented forces to deliver safety when a coordinated attack looms at our borders. That is why I am calling on all security agencies to put their differences, their egos, their desire for control, and their bank accounts aside, and allow the expertise and experience of NESA to dictate the response we need, if we are to survive as a peaceful, prosperous region.

"Mr. Patrick of Minutemen Arms has graciously ceded control of his forces to the militia structure of NESA, necessary for issuing orders that will prevent further death and destruction. Mr. Atlas of Atlas Protection has been hospitalized by the very same enemy – this is not the time to fight amongst ourselves and allow inexperienced security personnel to call the shots, in their own selfish attempts to promote their careers, or play hero. Some things are bigger than money, some events call for us to put aside our quarrels, and have faith in experienced leadership to keep us safe.

"NESA will not tolerate obstructionists while eradicating the cartel criminal element that has seeped into New England.

There may be no time for arbitration when any delay in justice will surely lead to unnecessary death, and could give the cartel the foothold it needs to expand permanently into New England, threatening our stability and economy. These are terrorists and must be treated as the invading enemy that they are. Justice cannot be served in the timeframe we *need* if they are treated like any old criminal. These methods may seem at times unorthodox, but trust me when I say they are necessary sacrifices if you wish to continue to live securely in peace.

"I ask you all to stay in your homes, and await instruction. In times of great crisis, it takes the collective to join hands and oppose evil which can be vanquished by no individual, by no disorganized band of profit seekers ready to exploit fears, even as the enemy closes in around them. Together, we can get through this. Together, we will keep this cartel from dragging us down, and instead, move forward!"

Drake finished, and the video cut out. A crowd of employees had gathered in his office to hear the address, and all looked at Drake with mesmerized adoration. Never had they known their boss to be so articulate, and such a fatherly leader. A slow clap started somewhere in the back, and grew to a loud applause. Cheers followed, and even Drake could not suppress a humble smile as employees shook his hand and patted him on the back.

"True leadership shines through in dark times!"

"Amazing speech sir, gave me chills."

Employees whispered to each other, how could they be worried with Drake in charge? They were so confident in his ability, and were thrilled to be a part of the company that would save New England. They had never been so proud to wear NESA badges. Emboldened by his speech, the employees returned to their posts to continue organizing.

Most other security companies seemed to be glad to have orders to follow, rather than be forced to deal with this crisis on their own. There was no precedent for an event like this, not the least of their problems including scared, frenzied customers. After all, they were used to petty criminals, not organized attacks by larger groups.

"Mr. Drake! You have to see this." His secretary, Benjamin, was frantically rushing toward Drake with a tablet in hand, pointing horrified at the screen.

It was a discussion board frequented by locals from southwestern New England, where the pods were being stopped. Criticism abounded of NESA, with reports of lies and exaggerations. One post read:

"I live right next to the station where all the pods are being rerouted. No drug cartels, just businessmen and women. I saw one guy get arrested after he refused to be detained in the station."

Another: "Where are the cartels streaming in that Drake's talking about?? All I see is everyday folks being harassed and manhandled by his thugs."

More: "Drake is a lying son of a bitch! He just committed a crime against every New Englander and should be held accountable! He needs to rot in a cell! DO NOT COMPLY! Alert your security company immediately if NESA cops try to use FORCE on you!"

"Oh just accept your authority and you'll save us? Thanks so much Drake, what would we do without you?" said with sarcasm. A serious tone followed, "The only thing I trust is my 30/30. I DARE those NESA thugs to push me around. No warrant? Shove it up your ass!"

"No druggies on the border. This is scary people. Remember your history lessons."

And worse still for Drake was that at least two smaller news outlets were already reporting on the lack of turmoil at the border. Drake tapped his finger against his desk, his jaw tight. He motioned for his secretary to leave and shut the door, then reached for his screen, and pressed some buttons.

The CEO of Coastal Internet appeared. "Mr. Drake, good morning."

"Good morning. My Agents will be coming to your offices soon. I need you to comply with them. I'm sending over the code for 100 ContraCoins. You should leave now and instruct your employees to follow their orders when they get there."

The CEO was silent at first, and he appeared to be in thought. The code arrived for the hundred ContraCoins: about $60,000. He glanced down at the codes, and pressed to collect them. Looking back at Drake, the CEO said gravely, "Please do everything you can to resolve this situation quickly," and disconnected.

Drake then quickly pressed more buttons.

"Yes sir?" A high ranking NESA officer appeared on the screen.

"Drug cartel members have taken over Coastal Internet, raid immediately, cut transmission, detain everyone; suspects are dressed in plain clothes and will be indistinguishable from the workers."

The officer gave a confused look, apparently not entirely believing Drake. "They... they're that organized sir?"

"This isn't some half-ass attack, this has been planned, officer. Now I need you to follow my orders. Raid and detain."

"Yes sir", the officer spoke slowly without confidence, "Should I... Should I wait for a warrant?"

Drake slammed his fist on his desk, and raised his voice, "Dammit there's no time! Do as you're told or I will find someone who will!"

"Yes sir! Right away!" and the officer changed his tune and immediately began to follow his orders.

Drake disconnected, and punched in another number. This time he had to bribe the editor of Post Daily to change the story and say that there were in fact cartel soldiers streaming into New England, but not on the pods, on the roads! Unfortunately Drake had to tip his hand in order to have the editor comply; he kept the details minimal, but offered the editor, in addition to money, an "unprecedented position with the power to review all media before it is disseminated to the public, in the interest of keeping damaging lies out of people's heads."

Arbiters were also calling Drake, furious that he was acting without permission or warrants. Most he ignored, but one hinted that he knew what was going on, and could offer his agency to cover Drake's actions, "in the interest of security, and the greater good of New England," of course.

The CEO of Collective Arbitration said he just wanted to be "rewarded" for his commitment to the security of New England, once the smoke cleared. Drake was glad to have warrants for all further actions, as his first attempt to issue orders without one was tense. And anyway, Barry was no longer around to become Minister of Arbitration. He sent along a warrant to placate the officer he had earlier ordered to raid Coastal Internet.

Drake was delighted to find that Mr. Patrick was already effectively using his power as Minister of Transportation. All pod transportation – except to and from hospitals, and for security companies – had been suspended inside of New England until further notice, with Minutemen Arms troops enforcing the freeze. They were also doing their best to keep the skies clear of pesky skyships and airplanes, and had closed major highways. The excuse was that a number of drug cartel soldiers had already infiltrated New England, and were going to muster to take out high level targets in order to collapse the security system, and set up their own criminal regime. News of New England seeded the proper story.

The media was doing its best to keep up with the details, but there was so much information to sort through, they ended up reporting whatever they could find. What the public got was a hodgepodge of misinformation, downright lies, and some truths; but only the truths that worked for Drake's needs. The editor he bribed was already testing out his position as Minister of Communications, and making up press releases which were taken as gospel by another 10 or so outlets. He also managed to use some of Drake's officers to remove certain websites, and block Internet access in more problem areas besides the southern coast.

It was only 9:00 in the morning, and so far things seemed to be materializing easily for Drake. But there were some notable exceptions. A large number of people from south central New England were not complying with the order to stay in their homes, and were busily communicating a resistance plan, according to NESA officers in the area.

Drake got his Minister of Resources on a video call and instructed her to cut the power to anyone she supplied in the trouble areas. He then sent a unit to close down another power plant that served the south central area, releasing reports that cartel members in the vicinity planned a devastating attack on the nuclear station. He blacked out power for 100,000 people, and reinforced the area with more patrols. This was, so it was reported, a hotbed area for cartel sleeper agents.

Drake knew that there would be countless more issues to deal with, so he sat in his office, prepared to issue more orders, and clean up more problems. In the meantime, he needed to put in motion his plan for when the smoke settled.

The Minister of Economics – who ran a New England-based charity that provided arbitration against corrupt businesses for those who could not afford it – was waiting outside his office, giddy with excitement, overflowing with ideas of how to best control New England's businesses, and how to best set in motion a plan for economic equality.

NINE

Atlas got a video call from his office. He jolted up in his hospital bed, and told the employee he would be in momentarily. As a nurse protested, Atlas removed the IV from his arm, and tore off the sensors monitoring his vitals.

"I'm sorry, thank you all so much, I'll be fine," he was saying to the nurse as he left the room. Molly was in the waiting area nodding off.

"What's going on?" she asked Atlas, yawning and stretching.

"Drake's taking control. He's trying to get all security to follow his orders because we are 'in a crisis.'" He made quotation marks with his fingers. They were walking swiftly down the hallway toward the non-emergency mag tube entrance in the hospital. "He mentioned me in a little speech he made. Said I was in the hospital, trying to act like we need to unify security in order to beat the threat from drug cartels. I need to get all my officers word that we are NOT playing along with this little game."

"Was this all Drake's plan?" Molly asked, exasperated.

"I don't know, but it sure is starting to seem like that. You should go check on Themis, make sure he knows what's going on. Let me know if he found out who the dead thug is, will you?"

"I'm on it," Molly said, with renewed vigor, taking a deep breath as the pod door closed behind Atlas. She started a brisk walk toward Themis's room.

His family members were all in various chairs sleeping with legs over the sides, and heads tilted in strange directions. Themis was on his tablet with an oxygen mask that was also administering small doses of various medicines to repair the lung tissue and dissolve the smoke residue. When Molly entered he removed his mask and smiled. Molly gave a nod back and quietly, so as not to wake his family, launched into an explanation of what she had just heard from Atlas.

Themis raised his hand to calm her. "I know, I am trying to get some evidence out to various arbitration agencies and security companies. Turns out that 'thug' was actually a Security Agent who went by Agent Orange – we don't know his real name. There's some evidence that he worked for Drake, and took contracts from others as well, it is just hard to trace due to the pay structure. Interestingly, the sunglasses he was wearing were able to block facial recognition, which is why last time we couldn't ID him and his partner leaving Barry's, but it's almost certain they are the same guys.

"The glasses are being analyzed to see if we can get any more info out of them, but it's high tech stuff, so I wouldn't be surprised if safeguards were built in to stop us. This *does* however connect Drake to Barry's murder, even though we would need more evidence for successful arbitration; but it will definitely help get some warrants to look into this further."

"But what about what's happening now? If Drake gets his way there won't be any arbiters left to go to!"

"Well, I am sending everything I have to Independent Arbitration since they are doing the review of the Barry Arbitration and Atlas Protection debacle. It doesn't hurt that they are pretty much the most influential arbiters in New England. I've sent along my notes too, linking your break-in with Barry's 'suicide' and the home invasion last night. I added my thoughts on where this whole power grab this morning is going, so hopefully they will take that into consideration – especially if I am right. I told them depending on how well this whole border/drug/terrorism crisis goes for Drake, he'll suggest rationing food and water, and moving to one currency."

"How do you figure that?" Molly asked.

"Well... I admit it is a bit of a stretch," Themis explained, "But Drake's actions this morning will not be taken lightly. He is all in: unless he holds onto the policing power he's attempted to grab this morning, he will certainly be arrested."

"But people won't go along with it, will they?" Molly's heart was pounding, and she couldn't understand why Themis seemed so calm.

Themis shrugged. "Unfortunately CCS instructed their street divisions to defer to NESA judgments if they come into contact with them. I think they are just trying to avoid any confrontations, but it could be bad news – sure is a bad precedent. And Drake's got one arbiter on his side, which I didn't see coming, but Collective Arbitration has already issued about a dozen warrants for NESA. The benefits of having investigatory database clearance," Themis added at Molly's questioning glance.

"Well, shouldn't we be out doing something about this?" Molly asked concerned.

Themis pointed to his tablet, "I'm doing everything I can from here, and it's a safer distance too," he managed a half-hearted smile. "Nights like last night, they put things in perspective. I've got a family, and I need to be here for them. Times like these you've got to keep calm. Chaos is exactly what Drake is depending on; panic."

"You're right," Molly replied, a bit calmer, "And I've got to do everything I can do, too. After all, action is the proper fruit of knowledge," and she smiled, a sort of confident yet cautious, modest smile.

"Where did you hear that?" Themis asked, letting out a couple of chuckles and a cough.

"I read it from a fortune cookie. I'm going down to the office, I'm going to start telling anyone who will listen what's really going on. Stay in contact!"

As Atlas got to his office, his employees descended on him, trying to figure out what to do. Atlas held up his hand to quiet his staff.

"First things first. Tell all field units that the only orders they should be listening to will come from this office. NESA is not in charge, and NESA will be held accountable for their actions in violating our customers' contracts. If that doesn't answer your questions, please see me in my office."

Some employees hurried back to their desks and some lined up at Atlas's door.

"We have a unit on 84 responding to an AP customer who claims he is being harassed by NESA troops. It's a standoff right now. He's in his car, we got a unit with guns drawn yelling to us for guidance, and NESA keeps calling more officers to the scene. It's about 25 to 10 right now." Atlas' secretary had made her way to the front and was briefing him.

"Do we have a skyship in the area? Let's get full surveillance of the situation. Tell our officers to try to get the customer on his way; if they can't, let's get an overruling on the warrant they have for the stop. Tell them not to do anything until we have eyes on the scene." She walked briskly out to do as he said.

Another employee came in. "Mr. Atlas, we have a complaint that one of our customers was detained while at work for Coastal Internet. He is accused of colluding with cartels to suppress Internet media. The raid took place before a warrant was issued, and no evidence has been forwarded to us."

"Are they still at their building?"

"He is being held at the regional NESA detainment center."

"Contact arbitration and send a team to the jail to free him. Let's see who else was detained too, and contact their security to see if we can work together on this."

"On it."

Molly was trying to decide how to go about alerting people to Drake's true intentions. She wanted to tell everything she knew, but some of it could not yet be verified with evidence. Overwhelmed by the events of the morning and the inquiries coming in, her boss essentially handed the reins to Molly.

"Put whatever you need to on the homepage, Molly. People need to be informed, and you're in the position to do it," Otto said. So Molly got to work.

Molly wrote:

Do we have all the information about what is really happening with NESA and Mr. Drake? No, and BER doesn't claim to. This is simply my account of what has happened over the past three weeks.

It started with my investigation into Barry Arbitration. There were some red flags to begin with, but BER standards for an ethical downgrade were met when evidence surfaced that Mr. Barry had accepted a personal bribe. All the information was on my personal devices, accounts, and safe drive. The article was due out in just days, today in fact, and BA was likely to go under.

I got a knock on my door the night of Saturday, September 26th, and I answered it, not knowing what was about to happen to me. I suffered a violent home invasion and attempted murder at the hands of a supposed drug cartel member who was following orders to kill me, due to my investigations into the drug cartel he worked for. The only problem; I have never in my career investigated any drug cartel. Business Ethics Review focuses on corruption in legitimate businesses; not on organizations who make their money through extortion and turf wars.

But there was someone who stood to gain from my death, and the disappearance of my devices: Barry Arbitration. Pains were taken to obscure the true purpose of the attempt on my life, but it now appears to have been a trade between Reed Barry and Cole Drake, CEO of New England Security Agency.

Barry Arbitration made the claim that Atlas Protection had manufactured evidence, a claim hotly disputed and under review by Independent Arbitration. But we do know that Mr. Barry had accepted bribes in the past, casting doubt on the truthfulness of the claims against AP.

Atlas Protection is a main competitor of NESA, and takes more fleeing customers from NESA than any other security company. This is the nature of the trade between Mr. Drake and Mr. Barry. But when Mr. Drake did not hold up his end of the bargain, Mr. Barry went from an accomplice to a liability for Mr. Drake.

The evening of Mr. Barry's murder – it is true it was not a suicide – Mr. Barry had visited Mr. Drake at his NESA office. Later that night, Agents were seen leaving Mr. Barry's house around the time of his death. One of those Agents has been identified with a high probability as having worked for Mr. Drake. Last night that Agent and his partner invaded and burned down the home of Officer James Themis, lead investigator of violent crimes at Corner Cop Security, in an attempt on his life. This has already been cast in the media as a drug cartel hit, just as was the attempt on my life, and the murder of Mr. Barry.

Since these agents have no known connection to drug cartels, and a probable connection to NESA, evidence suggests cartels are merely a scapegoat for the actions of Mr. Drake.

This morning's power grab by Mr. Drake further casts doubt on the drug cartel story, and highlights a desire for control and the retention of a fading business as Mr. Drake's motives.

I realize this is not a typical BER publication, nor does the evidence mentioned hold up to the usual standards of beyond reasonable doubt. However under the circumstances, and with such dire consequences, this information must be discussed prematurely, before it is too late. What is crystal clear, however, is that NESA has violated the rights of countless citizens today, in the name of securing the region. Please check back as more updates follow.

Molly felt strange posting such an incomplete article, as BER staked their reputation on accuracy of facts, and non-circumstantial evidence. But she was worried about what would happen if people did not know the truth. Three people had been attacked so far at Drake's command, with others caught in the crossfire. How many more would die or be maimed if she waited to amass evidence beyond a reasonable doubt?

Drake had shown his willingness to use force to get his way, and Molly was well aware of the danger she was in. Already she had survived two assassination attempts. If Drake solidified control of New England and created a border, her life would again be in jeopardy. But at least it would be difficult for Drake to take action against her when people heard the accusations; further attempts on her life would arouse even more suspicion and risk proving her claims. Then again, if Drake was successful in bringing New England under his control, he would be able to do away with Molly and her whistle-blowing without any consequences if she remained in the area.

She was risking her career, and indeed her life, but the future and freedom of New England was at stake. She knew she had to act. So Molly pressed submit, and the article appeared on the homepage. Drake would be tried in the court of public opinion. Molly hoped the market would respond properly.

Drake was furious that the article had been up for an hour before he was told. Jay and Hunter sat at the far side of Drake's desk, in the low chairs, terrified. Drake didn't yell, he didn't swear, he just stared from one to the other, jaw clenched, from time to time grinding his teeth. Jay was sweating noticeably.

"I would have told you sooner," he stammered, "but I was only informed a half hour ago," he shot an accusing glance at Hunter, seated on his left, who swallowed hard, "and... I thought I could get BER to take it down."

Drake was silent as he drew in a long breath through his nose and let it out, still staring from his droopy eyes, cheeks more bulldog-esque than ever, keeping eye contact that burned through Jay.

Jay nervously continued his failing explanation after a few unbearable silent seconds that seemed like an eternity.

"I mean, it's totally unsubstantiated..." he attempted a lighthearted, broken chuckle which was just short bursts of air and a half-hearted smirk, "their reputation..." Jay trailed off as he wiped the grin off his face, swallowed hard, and retreated back into silence, brow furrowed, to wait out the death stare from Drake.

Another eternity in seconds passed before Drake finally sighed and turned his chair, breaking the eye contact, to the immense relief of Jay and Hunter.

"Get the cameras. I need to make another statement," Drake ordered without expression. The two employees hurried out of the office.

Once on camera, streamed to News of New England's live feed, for the second time that day, Drake addressed viewers.

"As many of you know, I have always respected the information presented by Business Ethics Review, which has long supported ethical business practices. This is why I was disappointed to learn of a shoddy, unsubstantiated post by BER to their homepage. This post cast aside the usual guidelines used by BER to establish fact-based substantive reporting, instead relying on rumors and wild conjectures to cast myself, my business, and my tragically deceased friend Mr. Barry as corrupt criminals who would murder for profit.

"I call on Business Ethics Review to remove this defamatory and baseless post, and explain to the public why their trust should continue to be put in BER after such a sophomoric display of reporting. NESA has done nothing but make New England safer, standing up today for the people of New England against a grave threat of the unbridled invasion of drug cartels, just as this company, led by my grandfather, stood up to Unified New America when they invaded New England some 60 years ago.

"The actions of BER have put New Englanders at risk by downplaying the very real threat we face today from the cartels, and selfishly obstructing the mission of NESA in an attempt to grab headlines. NESA will not allow fringe conspiracy theories to undermine the security of our customers, and everyone else whom we have selflessly agreed to protect in this time of crisis.

"Thank you for believing in the honorable mission of NESA, and standing with us in this fight against cartel terrorism. BER has shown today it seeks only to divide, while you and I know that when it comes to making New England safe, together we can."

As Drake spoke, an article appeared from News of New England titled, "Have Drug Cartels Infiltrated New England Media?" as another reporter for NNE spoke on camera about the possibility that New York cartels had been planning a takeover of New England for some time, and could easily have entrenched sympathizers in media outlets, banks, security agencies, and everywhere else. "Was the attack on Molly Metis staged?" asked another outlet, "so that a supposed victim could divert blame away from the cartels and toward the strongest security company rivaling cartel insurgency?"

Other news outlets didn't take this story as fact, however it obscured the story from BER since most news debates began to surround the idea of whether or not cartels had infiltrated New England and to what degree. Molly's theory, published on BER, was not as widely discussed by the mainstream outlets, though some speculated on why BER would publish such conspiracy theories.

But again some media and online commenters could not all be fooled, and many voiced their opposition to NESA's actions, and supported the BER story Molly had written. Even if it is shoddy reporting, she had plenty of reason to draw those conclusions, they said. This prompted yet another raid of an Internet Service Provider by NESA. Drake couldn't shut down BER or remove the story without creating a bigger mess, so he tried to black out the areas of New England most opposed to NESA rule, with help from his Minister of Resources and her influence on the power grid.

This also involved more bribes, more sold positions for the coming government, and more trumped up charges for dissenters. Atlas Protection was the only company actively opposing the violations of contract by NESA. Everyone else was following the orders of Drake, or just doing nothing.

At this point, his orders were not entirely unreasonable. Drake had his own NESA forces carrying out any sketchy raids or enforcement, while other companies who had yielded control were mostly patrolling and policing the few actual crimes and unrest that had taken place over the course of the day. The heavy militarized presence, and supposed threat from cartels had convinced most people to just stay inside and wait it out.

Benjamin remained by Drake's side to update him as any pertinent information came into NESA headquarters. Most other employees were kept in the dark, believing that NESA was actually fighting a dangerous threat to their freedom.

"There's a small security agency refusing to follow the orders issued by NESA." Benjamin paused, frowning slightly, and looked to Drake for a response.

Drake was staring off, not looking at anything in particular, and fidgeting with a cigar lighter in his left hand. "Let's get a warrant issued for the CEO for conspiring with the cartels to violate select contracts. Arrest him, and disperse his employees with the threat of arrest if they continue to carry out their roles as employees of the agency."

Benjamin made a note, and continued, "We have several standoffs with Atlas Protection at this point. But they are too big to deal with the same as the smaller agencies."

"What happened with the highway standoff?" Drake asked.

Benjamin summarized for Drake all the information he had gathered.

The original motorist whom NESA pulled over was allowed to leave, but Atlas Protection units and NESA units remained on the scene, each trying to serve arrest warrants. NESA Agents managed to detain a handful of AP units through the use of flashbangs and smoke grenades, while the other Atlas Protection units had been cornered, just off the highway.

As the NESA detainee transport vehicle departed the scene, more AP units who had set up post a quarter-mile down the road threw a spike strip across the lane. The tires blew out on the transport truck, it skidded sideways, almost regained control, and then skid into the center barrier with the back of the vehicle slamming into a mag tunnel pole.

AP then swarmed the vehicle and detained the NESA units, transporting them and the freed AP detainees out of the area via skyship. When the skyship arrived at the hospital the AP police were taken in to check on their injuries from the crash, but before the NESA captives could be transported to an AP detainment facility, more NESA Agents stepped in, commandeered the skyship, and detained the remaining AP crew.

Drake gave a satisfied nod. Benjamin continued to give him all the relevant information.

Units from each company had also clashed at the detention center where Coastal Internet employees were being held, after Atlantic Arbitration refused to accept the warrants issued by Collective Arbitration. The situation unfolded similarly to the standoff on the highway. NESA Agents detained Atlas Protection units, before being thwarted and detained themselves.

"Everyone's been smart enough so far not to use lethal force," added Benjamin. "It just seems like it is only a matter of time until something goes wrong, and gets violent. When you got all these Agents with loaded guns being aimed at each other, and military equipment being used," Benjamin shrugged. "I think patience is wearing thin."

Drake had the information he needed, and was done listening to his secretary's commentary.

"Thank you Benjamin, that will be all."

Arbitration agencies would usually work these problems out without incident, but NESA's arbiter was following none of the usual procedure. Adding to the problem was the fact that some arbitration agencies could not even function, since employees could not reach work through roads and mag tunnels, and others could not work remotely due to certain Internet and power blackouts, orchestrated by NESA, yet blamed on the cartels.

It seemed the media was having trouble teasing apart what had been caused by NESA, and what they had solved. News teams were on the scene when NESA Agents got one power plant back up and running. News teams had not been on the scene three hours earlier when NESA Agents had raided the plant and cut the power output.

Of course, this gridlock posed another problem for New England, where normal life had now been stopped for almost 12 hours. Since NESA was now in the business of solving problems, this just helped them get poised for the next phase, taking control as they "reopened" New England. Food shipments needed to resume (many were held at the border controlled by NESA), people needed to get to work and get their Internet back, in order to work from home.

Power outages had also posed problems for regular activities, especially with most transportation relying on electricity. Many people didn't know that NESA had directly caused the power outages, the Internet blackouts, the gridlock on the mag tunnels, the impasse on the highways, and the stoppage of travel, imports, and exports at the borders of New England. But they knew that NESA kept saying, and the media repeating, that it could get everything solved and going again. New England residents just had to trust in NESA, and by the time of tomorrow morning's commute, the pods in the mag tunnels would be running on time.

Some of the few arbiters that were able to stay open despite the turmoil had issued rulings and warrants against NESA. But since NESA had control of the vast majority of street forces in New England, there was no one to enforce these warrants, except an already overwhelmed Atlas Protection. NESA also said that all new arbitration rulings between security agencies would be suspended until everything was resolved, since arbiters were not functioning as they should, meaning NESA's arbiter could issue warrants against other companies that ran power, Internet, and shipping, but other company's arbiters couldn't issue a ruling or warrant against NESA or any other security agency. This inadvertently helped AP avoid major warrants against it by Collective Arbitration, though some warrants had been issued before the NESA decree limiting further warrants.

Law was in a jumble as NESA tried to keep the appearance of legitimacy, while really doing anything they wanted. The appearance, however, was extremely important, at least until control could be solidified, and they could scale back the posturing. To instill confidence in NESA, Drake decided that he would coordinate all power and Internet to be turned back on, just in time for an address by himself to the people of New

England. Like the earlier addresses, Drake assumed media outlets would focus on his words; so it was just a matter of creating the right talking points to keep people distracted from the real events and facts.

Drake needed to strike a balance. After his speech people needed to be alarmed enough to only discuss what he had said, ignoring other news items that would pop up.

Taking advantage of the distraction, Drake intended to send Agent White to lead an assault against Atlas headquarters. Of course the assault would be blamed on drug cartels, but some people would obviously see the connection between Drake's desire to monopolize New England's security forces, and the destruction of the only remaining adversary to NESA's control. But if properly framed, Drake knew he could make the attack on Atlas headquarters into the smoking gun he needed, killing two birds with one stone.

If he initiated, and quelled, an attack on his own NESA headquarters as well, Drake assumed he would successfully throw off the trail. Then, if the right targets at Atlas Protection were taken out, the two agencies could "come together" to finally once and for all "stop the cartels." After all, once they were both attacked, it would seem as if they faced the same enemy, and the public would eat it up if NESA and AP joined forces for the greater good. But this was not going to happen with Kitt Atlas calling the shots at AP.

Agent White had remained in the same bar until the sun came up, drinking his worries away. Despite his training and professional demeanor, White could not shake the sadness that accompanied the death of his longtime partner and only friend. Not that he generally did much talking, or sharing of feelings, but the one person on earth that he could truly open up to was now gone. White didn't want to go back to the house that the two agents owned far north in New England. He didn't want to step foot back into the adap that the two kept near the coast, or the adap they shared in south central New England. If he went home alone, it would just compound the sadness. So far he could keep the worst feelings at bay with alcohol.

Some people in his position – having lost the most important person in their life – might feel anger, but his logical brain fought these emotions. White's philosophy was that if you play with fire, you're going to get burned. He had been burned before, but now he felt charred. Stumbling out of the pub with light poking over the horizon, White squinted at the sun, as if trying to discern if it really was morning already; he didn't think to put his sunglasses back on. After swaying to the left and grabbing a railing for stabilization, he lunged right and started meandering along the sidewalk, periodically touching the brick building for support as he swayed.

Agent White took the conveyors as far as they would bring him, and then continued walking like a zombie without any destination. He smelled strongly of alcohol, and drew judgmental glances from anyone that passed – though relatively few people were out and about due to the events that were unfolding.

White still wore his "drug cartel" disguise, except he had discarded his sweatshirt in order to change his appearance slightly. He took the most rural road he could find, and started walking. Maybe it was ten minutes or it could have been two hours, but finally he found a tempting field, and influenced by the booze in his system, he cut off the road and wobbled toward a hilltop, bare of trees. Agent White sloshed through the runoff in the ditch at the edge of the street, filled with weeds, mud, and stagnant greenish water. He managed to get over a very old barbed wire fence with only some minor scratches, and continued stumbling through the long grass toward the hill. The sun had not yet reached its peak and there was still dew weighing down the grass.

The expression on his face had remained blank since he left the bar, except for an occasional squint, or wetting of his lips. He looked and felt like Trix did when he took the drug to induce apathy – but White wasn't on any drugs, except alcohol. He got to the top of the hill, and slowly spun around, looking out across a field, then toward the road, gazing over the forest to the west, and seeing buildings in the distant east.

After a couple rotations he stopped when the sun was to his back, and in one fluid motion that was more graceful than a collapse, he laid down on the moist grass with his arms outstretched. For a while he watched the clouds, which might have been spinning a bit extra from the alcohol still coursing through his veins. After a half hour, his eyes started to close, but would periodically shoot open again. Finally, as noon approached, he fell asleep, and there he remained until Drake woke him up with a call to his sunglasses, which had remained tucked in his pants pocket since entering the bar the night before.

Agent White heard the beeping first. Jolting his head up, he looked around, forgetting where he had fallen asleep. The sun had just set, and darkness was beginning to close in. On the western horizon a bright orange glow could still be seen, that reminded White of the fire from the night before. It told him that the darkness closing in on him would not go away with tomorrow's rising sun. His eyes were still adjusting as he reached for his sunglasses, and put them on to answer the call.

His voice was low and hoarse as he first tried to answer, so White cleared his throat and then repeated, "Yeah?"

"White, I need something else from you." Drake said before adding as an afterthought in a concerned tone, "Are you okay?"

There was a short pause while White drew in a breath and let it go, then cleared his throat once more before answering, "Yeah I'm fine. What do you need?"

Drake paused in turn, deciding if he should continue or if White had been through enough. Drake really didn't have anyone else to go to at this point however, so he continued.

"I need another drug cartel attack. This time at Atlas headquarters. Can you scrounge together a few guys who look the part? Take them with you? And send a few to NESA headquarters as well... more incompetent ones though, maybe harder drug users, that no one will miss."

"I can do that. Any targets? How do you want it done?"

"It just needs to look like an attack designed to shut down the central office of AP so that they can't control their street units. It would be great if Atlas was killed in the process. But just destroying the equipment, making sure they can't function normally will be sufficient... obviously if you get Atlas, there will be a bonus, say a hundred grand worth of ContraCoin. And at NESA headquarters, I just need them to get in the front door and I'll take care of them." Drake paused again and then added, "After you finish, take a vacation. I'd say you earned some time off."

White signed off without another word.

Agent White heaved himself to his feet, and brushed off some grass and twigs that were on his pants and the back of his shirt. He started walking down the hill in the direction of the road, activating the GPS on his glasses to find his location. He was 4 miles from the nearest mag tunnel. He started walking, the same expressionless look on his face he wore that morning when he was walking down the smooth ceramic road in the other direction.

While he walked he contacted some people he knew that would join him on a job for the right price. Remembering the trouble he and Agent Orange got themselves into the night before, White decided to get a bigger gang together. He could afford to pay them well and still have the majority of the reward for himself. Then he found three useful idiots to storm NESA headquarters, offering them enough money to make sure they were interested: they would never be able to collect anyway.

White figured that once this job was done, maybe he'd shoot out to the west coast on a mag pod to clear his head. Heavy drinking coupled with minor drug use and anonymous sex might make him feel better. New England winter loomed, and hanging out on the beach sounded appealing. He hadn't taken a real vacation in years – it distracted him from his work, which he admittedly loved, until last night.

Now his thoughts were jumbled, and his attention to detail compromised by the distractions from Agent Orange's death. They say you don't know what you've got until it's gone. Agent White just now realized how much Agent Orange truly meant to him. They worked together in the day, and went home together every night. White asked himself how he could have been so stupid not to appreciate the life he had, destroyed in one fell swoop.

As he dwelled on it sober, his sadness did turn to brief anger, but not at Officer Themis who had fired the fatal shot; at Drake who had given them the assignment. *I'm a skilled agent*, he thought, *not some jackbooted thug*. But he could have said no, and he knew it. White had made his bed, now he had to lie in it... alone.

Drake was preparing for his third televised address of the day. His plan was to comfort supporters, scare dissenters, and keep everyone else distracted and in debate. Not the true debate – is it NESA or the drug cartels to blame for the instability in New England? – but the debate which he would implant in the people's minds: are Drake's ideas good or bad?

Instead of letting people discuss, "is it better to be free, can we trade freedom for security, and can initiating force ever be moral?" he would change the discussion to, "is one currency good or bad? Will using blanket force benefit me or not?" People would be distracted from the philosophical implications of the actions they accepted from NESA, and instead debate individual issues in a vacuum, as if NESA's means would be justified, as long as the ends were positive.

Drake knew the means could not be separated from the ends. Of course, he didn't really care about the ends for anybody other than himself. But he knew some would justify the actions of NESA, arguing that if their monopoly on force eventually turned out to benefit the masses, then it would be a good thing.

Drake was too smart to believe his own lies. *You'll know the tree by the fruit it bears*, he thought, laughing in his head at the peasants of New England. *A society built on force cannot yield peace.* But millions of sheep were all Drake needed to acquire the power he always desired to replace the love he lost. The power to use force as he saw fit, in stark contrast to the power he currently wielded, to use force only in response to force; and use money, almost exclusively in non-aggressive pursuits.

A couple of Drake's employees doted on him to make sure he looked good for the final address of the evening. His tie was straightened, what little hair he had put in place, and the lights turned on. Drake cleared his throat, and tried to ignore the pang of nerves and throbbing sound of blood in his ears.

"People of New England, I will not abandon you. Tomorrow New England will resume its normal day-to-day business, but in safety, unintimidated by the drug cartel threat that has entrenched itself in New England, but will soon be eradicated, with the dedication of NESA and all other deputized security companies. But society does not magically organize itself, and we cannot eradicate this threat without banding together. Unity is what we need, together New England will stand against the drug cartels, divided we will fall.

"So I propose hitting the enemy where it hurts, in their wallet. New England Security Agency proudly boasts a strong currency, easily traceable, and therefore not in use by the worst elements of our society; the people who violate others' rights. Starting tomorrow, NESA currency, issued by Bank of New England, will become the standard currency of New England. Other currencies will be converted into BONEs, and a deadline will be set when all exchanges will only accept BONE notes. People need not lose their savings, simply convert before the deadline, and nothing will change.

"Due to today's upsets caused by the drug cartels, it will take some time for the market to work out the kinks. To solve this problem and ensure no one goes without necessities such as food and water, I have arranged for an expert to set all prices for water and food, as well as manage its distribution, until further notice. This will mean equitable distribution of resources that belong to all of us, to make sure the drug cartels do not achieve their goal of disrupting our happy and fruitful New England lives.

"Thanks to the work of New England Security Agency's dedicated staff and agents, all power and Internet has been restored to New England, and those responsible have been detained. They are awaiting charges, and their links to the drug cartels are being investigated. Again, this effort to return our region to peace will require the cooperation of everyone. Many cartel members have not yet been found out, and are embedded in every facet of our markets. Don't mistake clean-cut individuals for being innocent. Even those who abstain from drugs can be guilty of the murder and turmoil that accompanies cartelization. To them, it is not about the drugs, it is about the control and power that comes from infiltrating our society.

"Keep this in mind, that it is not only the dirty and debilitated who work for the cartels. Your neighbors, your kids' teachers, your arbiters, or your co-workers could be involved for profit. That is why it is so important that if you see something, you say something. NESA has set up operators to take down your concerns, which can be submitted on our website, or through face-to-face conversations if you call the NESA office. Together we will clean up New England, and emerge stronger as a community. Remember: NESA never sleeps, so that you can."

Staff around the room nodded their heads in approval as Drake finished and the feed cut out. They were impressed by how their previously ordinary boss had risen to such an occasion. How special and proud those employees felt that they were part of the company that would save New England.

Ten

As Drake finished his address, two employees of Independent Arbitration looked at each other with raised eyebrows, perturbed. They were surrounded by screens, evidence, and documents full of information concerning Drake, NESA, the attempted murder of Molly Metis, the attack and arson at Themis's house, Barry Arbitration, Barry's suicide *or murder*, and Atlas Protection. There was a smart screen with notes written all over it, and lines connecting various names and tidbits. There were various scenarios laid out, and there were percentages written next to each one, calculated based on their likelihood.

The two employees had rolled their eyes when they got the pile of information from Themis earlier in the day. They knew he was onto something, but thought his personal feelings were getting in the way of rationality in this case. Now his prediction that Drake would attempt to transition to a single currency had come true, and Themis's scenario seemed more plausible.

After holding each other's questioning stare for a few moments in surprise, the older man with disheveled graying hair pressed a button on one of the telescreens to contact his superior. The solid woman with shoulder length dirty blond hair, focused her thoughts on one of the screens. She confirmed the single currency prediction, which increased Themis's scenario to the highest probability percentage of any others.

"Sir," the middle aged man said to his boss on the telescreen, "I think you should take a look at this."

Agent White switched off the feed in his sunglasses when Drake's speech finished. He was zooming through a mag tunnel toward Atlas headquarters accompanied by seven dirty, sketchy people who looked the part of low level drug cartel soldiers. White was silent, but a couple of the thugs carried on sordid conversations about hookers, back alley dealings, and drug use.

There were a couple of blocks to walk after they got out of the pod, but the streets were like a ghost town. It was dark out except for some lights illuminating the street, and a few lit windows in the buildings. The Atlas Protection headquarters was the brightest, and biggest building around, standing six stories. It was obvious that operations had not much slowed down for the night; White could see people hurrying past windows.

Agent White had explained his plan of attack to the thugs while in transit. First, a team of four would go in guns blazing, throwing small explosives and flashbangs, taking out any cameras they could find. Two would stay outside to hold off any squads that responded, although most Atlas street units were still caught in standoffs with NESA police, and the others were stretched to their limit. Either way it would likely be a good chunk of time before help showed up, and by then Agent White and his team planned to be gone. Agent White omitted the probability that the team would leave slightly smaller than it arrived.

The remaining two "thugs," White being one of them, would follow a minute or two behind the initial team, to catch anyone off guard who might think they could sneak up on the original raiding team of four. If things got too heavy, White would retreat with whoever was left. They wanted to be in and out in under 20 minutes, and destroy enough of the building in the process to shut down operations for at very least, 12 hours. That would give NESA enough of an advantage to consolidate control, and gain the upper hand on the standoffs. Best case scenario, Atlas would die, and NESA could "unite" with AP.

The gang of eight stopped outside on the sidewalk, and White gave a nod to the four designated initial attackers – the craziest, strongest, and most violent of the bunch. One smiled like a pirate, complete with a couple of gold teeth, and pulled a large submachine gun from his jacket. Another gave a weird, apparently joyful, grimace that looked like he was in slight pain while pulling a shotgun from his jacket that made White wonder how it possibly could have fit under even the long trench coat. The other two 20-something year olds who looked more clean cut than the rest, and wore all black, simply nodded stoically, each brandishing large handguns with extended magazines, and tactical gear-packs on their backs. The last two operated as a team, which made Agent White jealously hope that one or both would die, adding to his reasons for sending them in first.

The pirate-like thug led the way, kicking the front door open and entering the lobby. Kicking the door was unnecessary since it was unlocked, but it made him feel cooler. From the sidewalk, White heard the submachine gun going off, and then the shotgun pumping out two booming shells. An alarm sounded and the building appeared to go into lockdown mode, with some windows being obscured by metal shutters. The front door clicked locked, but since it was glass, it didn't make much difference for the men still outside.

On the top floor the operations room had shut and locked with most employees inside, including Mr. Atlas. From there, operations of all AP units and patrols were controlled, and every camera, automatic door, and other defense mechanism of the building could be accessed and manipulated.

The employees that were not able to get to the safe control room hid in their offices. The security guards on the first floor had been taken by surprise, one killed when riddled with bullets from the submachine gun, the other dying slowly after taking a burst of shotgun pellets to the chest. The first floor secretary managed to slip out a side door unnoticed after sounding the alarm. The two partner gunmen with pistols disappeared somewhere in the building after slipping into the stairwell. As they climbed the stairs, they took out all the cameras in sight, and quietly exited the stairwell onto the roof.

The shotgun-wielding gunman was finding every window or glass doored office and surveying it for any unlucky employees. The first one he peppered was an employee who went down, but was not seriously wounded. She laid still under her desk as he moved on to the next glass-encased office.

Here, he pumped a few shells in the direction of the desk a man was hiding behind. When he got to the next office though, bullets came flying out at him before he could get a shot off. The gunman with the shotgun took two rounds to the chest and one to the forehead, collapsing against a wall and sliding down, smearing blood as he slid. His head wobbled back and forth before resting on his right shoulder.

The man with the submachine gun saw this happen, and emptied his magazine in that general direction, while keeping a safe distance. He didn't see or hear movement, so he decided to move on; he wasn't going to get close enough to find out more. As he got to the second floor, everything was very quiet. He poked his head into the hallway, but didn't see any employees, or anything else of much interest. He figured the higher the floor, the more damage could probably be done, so he continued onto the third.

There were no people in sight, but on the right the gunman saw a lot of expensive looking high tech equipment. He tossed a grenade down the hallway, sending shrapnel into computers, tablets, telescreens, cameras, and a couple gadgets he could not recognize. Smoke started pouring out of a few of the machines, so he took a left down the hallway, blazing away at anything that looked like an expensive target, since there were not any human targets in sight.

As he turned the corner at the opposite end of the hall a .50 caliber gun smoothly and abruptly descended from the ceiling, turned rapidly with a slight whining sound, toggled onto the target, and sent three rounds in quick succession into the center of the submachine gun-wielding pirate-like man. BA-BA-BOOM.

As the bullets tore into him they took chunks out of his torso, leaving gaping holes and sweeping him off his feet, sending him flying into a glass window, which immediately shattered, having cracked from the bullets, allowing his body to exit the building and plummet three floors to slam into the sidewalk below in front of the building. The time from the gun descending from the ceiling to the thug hitting the pavement could not have been more than four seconds.

Agent White watched the body fall, back first, and thud onto the pavement, hearing the unmistakable sound of snapping bones and wet sploosh like a water balloon popping.

"I think that's our cue," joked White dryly to the thug who would accompany him inside. The thug swallowed hard, much more nervous than he felt a few minutes ago. "Send me a message if a unit arrives," White said to the remaining two gunmen on the sidewalk.

In the secured operations room the .50 cal operator who wore a slight smirk and could have been a Spartan warrior if he was born at the right time, turned to a serious Mr. Atlas who was standing behind him arms crossed, and quipped, "In retrospect, we probably should have put that .50 cal in a hallway with a better backstop than a window."

Mr. Atlas gave an uncomfortable chuckle as he shook his head. Turning to another operator, he said, "Let's try to funnel them to other defenses, lock all A1 doors and unlock all D1's and D2's. Where's our responding unit?"

"Six blocks out sir, but they are making a detour, NESA has set up a roadblock."

"What? We don't have a skyship in the area?" Atlas spat.

"No sir, three are out of commission, and the closest one in engaged with NESA troops 26 kilometers out."

"Well tell them to disengage; that can wait. We need backup ASAP!"

Six floors below, Agent White and the nervous thug with him had shattered the glass on the front door, and ducked into the building. They stepped over the dead guards, and White peered around the corner to see the shotgun-wielding thug dead and slumped up against the wall. Momentarily bullets came flying in White's direction, exploding a fire extinguisher on the wall. He ducked back, and motioned for the nervous thug to lay down cover fire. As he did, White safely rolled to the stairwell, followed by his accomplice. The first flight they climbed with White aiming his gun up, and the young thug making sure no one followed from the first floor. The second floor door was locked, so they continued to the third, which was open.

White glanced into the hallway, where to the right something had been smoldering, but was now doused with white foam sprayed down from a knob in the ceiling. To the left there was shattered glass and White understood this to be the window that the pirate-y thug was slammed through by bullets. And guessing that there wasn't an employee running around with a handheld cannon, White decided not to risk going down that hallway. Instead they continued to the fourth floor, which was locked, and then the fifth floor, which was not. Agent White sent the other thug first through this door.

The thug walked into the hallway and looked around. He tried to open the door to the right, but it was locked. White motioned for him to continue down the hallway to the left, and followed a good 3 meters behind him. Before rounding the corner, the thug looked back at White like a scared child first riding a bike, begging his parents not to let go. White said nothing and made no movement, instead standing with knees bent, gun extended in a combat position. Swallowing hard, the thug turned and prepared himself to take the step around the corner.

But before he stepped into the other hallway, a pop was heard above him like a firecracker, and a cloud of red mist shot from the ceiling billowing out to form a reverse mushroom cloud as it hit the floor. It completely engulfed the thug and he let out a shrill scream, yelling "My eyes!" as he dropped his gun, and fell to the ground on his knees, hands over his face. "My eyes!" he repeated as he started to sob, his voice cracking. "I'm blind. Help me!" he yelled, but Agent White said nothing, just cautiously backed up. As Agent White doubled back to the stairwell the mist wafted down the hall.

He could hear gurgling and choking sounds coming from the hallway as he slammed the door, allowing the slightest mist to enter the stairwell, as the thug left behind continued to beg for White to help him. It was only a form of pepper spray, but even the bit that managed to escape into the stairwell with White made his eyes water like he was cutting onions and had touched his eyes with the juice. Agent White had to collect himself before continuing to the sixth floor. He could only imagine how much it stung for the thug he had abandoned, given the small amount White had come into contact with had such a strong effect.

As White suspected, the heavy steel door on the sixth floor was locked, so he took out the two sticky explosives he had brought, and placed them about where he thought the hinges were, on the other side. White descended the stairs a couple of flights, checking first to make sure the employee with a gun on the first floor hadn't come up behind. Then he toggled the detonator on his sunglasses, and set off the explosives. It was a deafening roar, not the least of which included the twisting screeching metal of the door. Bits of debris wafted down the middle of the stairwell past White. He waited a few moments for the smoke to clear.

By the time White ascended back to the top floor, white foam was already leaking through from behind the twisted metal door, sprayed from the other side. Not sure if this was automatic or a human that sprayed the fire retardant, for good measure Agent White pushed the twisted metal which had been the door aside just enough to roll a flashbang through. It exploded, and as White's ears rang for a moment he pushed the bottom half of the door open enough to squeeze into the sixth floor hallway. The top of the door had not come off its hinge, so only the bottom right corner could be pried open enough to make it through. The jagged metal of the door ripped White's shirt as he crawled through, and scraped his back deeply, drawing blood. There was no one on the other side, and the hallway was dark, with only a flickering exit sign lighting a small area where White crouched.

There were no other signs that the first wave of gunmen had entered this floor yet, and White wondered where the partners had gone. His sunglasses lit up with an alert. A responding AP unit had arrived on the scene, and moments later he heard an exchange of gunfire erupt outside. Before it ended, he decided he needed to make his move. White couldn't decide whether to get out now, or to first attempt to inflict more damage on the building, and possibly kill Atlas in the process, which would substantially increase his pay. Just when he decided to look for a back exit, White heard the muffled sound of something heavy clunking against thin metal, followed by an explosion. Then he heard another object clunking against metal, followed by a small pop, and the distant and muted sound of steam escaping.

A commotion quickly ensued from one hallway over on the same floor White was on; the top story. There was coughing and yelling, and then another clunking sound, followed by another hissing gas sound. On the roof, the two partner thugs were tossing their tear gas canisters into the vents which had been opened up by a grenade to ensure they would sufficiently leak the tear gas into the offices and command center.

In the secure control room, the tear gas was leaking out of the vents and enveloping the operators. Atlas was yelling to remain calm, as people dropped to the ground coughing. A sliding metal sound told White that someone was unlocking the secure room, and a man came running around the corner coughing, fleeing the gas. Agent White fired, and he thought he hit the man, who fell back bending at the knees and catching himself with his hands, before doing a crab-like walk to drag himself out of the line of fire. The woman who came immediately behind the first man gasped, and threw herself backwards avoiding another bullet sent by White toward the terrified Atlas Protection employees.

White heard a couple whispers, a click, and then something the size of a baseball flew from around the corner where the employees had come from, hit against the wall, and started rolling toward Agent White. White dove back through the twisted remnants of the door, but his right leg got caught on the jagged strip that had cut his back, and now dug into his calf, keeping his leg in the hallway as the flashbang exploded just inches away. As his vision went white for a second, he felt searing pain shoot up his shin. His ears rang worse than before, and his head throbbed more painfully than the most intense hangover. Yelling expletives White yanked his foot into the stairwell to find his left leg had been badly burnt below the knee to the point where blisters abounded, and one flap of skin appeared to be dangling and melted. His calf was bleeding from the jagged door's puncture wound, but it didn't look like anything major had been severed.

Agent White could hardly focus on anything but his agonizing injuries, until he heard the footsteps of someone quickly climbing the stairs a few floors below. Not quite sure what his next move would be, White buried the pain, and jumped to his feet, limping, looking around for the method used by the partner thugs to get to the roof. If they didn't have a plan of how to escape off the roof, White still liked his chances there better than trying to storm out the front door with Atlas units waiting outside.

White had to jump to reach the metal ladder which ascended through a vertical shaft toward the roof. It was usually blocked by a metal cage at the bottom, but this was left open by the others' bullets. Looking up, White was happy to see the roof hatch likewise left open, so he pulled himself up, and began to climb, babying his throbbing right leg.

A lead projectile clinked on the ladder and sprayed hot fragments of metal into White's hand a split second before he heard the gunshot from below. The footsteps had been the employee from the first floor firing up the stairwell at White. The other bullets didn't land as close, and White sped up his climb to the roof. The employee reloaded and climbed another set of stairs as White heaved himself out of the hatch and onto the gravel-covered roof, narrowly avoiding the next barrage of bullets from a few floors below, which whizzed into the air above the building.

On the roof, Agent White rolled onto his back, and took a moment to catch his breath before looking over to the partner thugs, who apparently had come well prepared. They were strapped into harnesses with black ropes attached, hammering anchors into the top of the roof. They saw White, but didn't bother waiting for him; their payment was in escrow and did not depend on White's survival.

In unison, the two jumped backwards off the side of the roof, and began to repel down the wall of the building.

Stumbling to his feet, White half crawled half limped to the front edge of the building, and looked over to see the bodies of the two thugs that were left outside to hold off the responding Atlas Protection unit. He could also see a group of three AP officers nursing one unit's wounds, and NESA cars turning onto the street, sirens blaring. Officially the NESA agents were responding to the AP distress call, but really they were doing everything they could to obstruct the AP team that had arrived despite NESA's best efforts.

Agent White did his best to run/limp to the side of the roof where the two thugs had repelled. In the distance he could make out a large white skyship drifting toward the roof. White took off his ripped bloody t-shirt, and wrapped it around one of the ropes, placing his hands around the wadded-up t-shirt. He moved to the side of the roof, and looked down, which he immediately realized was a mistake as his stomach lurched and his heart sank – he should have just taken the plunge. He gripped his t-shirt wrapped around the rope, alternating between a tight hold, and a loose grip, allowing himself to slide down the rope, guided by his feet, without the rope burning his hands.

About three or four stories above the ground level ally, the thug whose rope White had latched onto saw White, and yelled at him to get off the rope, since White's weight on the line was destabilizing him. Agent White ignored him, but the thug started to tug at the rope, and swing it back and forth to loosen White's hold. White's feet slipped, and he fell three meters before being able to once again grip the rope tightly enough through the t-shirt to stop his descent. Agent White grabbed the rope with his feet again, and gritting his teeth, let go with one hand to grab the knife in his pocket.

"Get off, you piece of shit!" The thug bellowed from below, but White again ignored him, and reached down in a crouching position so that his right hand could reach below where his feet and bent knees were tightly holding the rope.

Supporting his weight mostly with his left hand and feet, White ran his blade across the rope, swinging wildly to and fro, hardly able to keep from plummeting. Three more quick slashes with the blade, and the rope snapped before the thug below realized what was even happening. The thug screamed unintelligibly as he plummeted to the ground over 13 meters, landing on his back. His partner yelled wildly, and then proceeded to descend double time down his rope toward his friend.

White was then left hanging almost four stories up from a rope which he had cut from underneath himself. He caught his breath, and looked down to see the fallen thug writhing in pain; it surprised White that he had survived the fall and was still conscious. As the thug screamed in agony, White hoped he could make it to the ground before units in front of the building heard the pitiful cries of the crippled thug, and came to investigate.

White reaffirmed his grip on the rope, and placed his feet against the building. Taking a deep breath and clenching his jaw, he ran sideways across the wall until the rope was pulled tight, and he could run no further. He pushed off hard with all the might his legs could muster, reintroducing searing pain into his burnt and lacerated right leg. As he let go of the rope, he fell another three meters before reaching the intact rope of the second thug. Grabbing at that line, White slipped even further down, almost losing his grip twice as his stomach dropped with him, his hands sliding over the rope with no t-shirt to stop the burn. Flesh was ripped off his left hand, but stayed on, forming a bloody flap, as White finally stabilized himself on the rope, two floors above the ground.

The second thug was just reaching the ground and unhitching himself from the rope. He ran over to his fallen friend, and threw himself to his knees next to him, trying to help, knowing full well there was nothing he could do. Nevertheless this gave White the opportunity to descend the rest of the rope in peace, babying his torn hand, burnt bleeding leg, and sore right hand embedded with lead shrapnel from the bursting bullet spray.

White quickly surveyed his surroundings once down in the alley next to the building where the unharmed thug tended to his fallen partner. He was surprised that still no units had surrounded the building, and guessed this was due to the obstruction of NESA troops. Catching his breath, White turned away from the thugs, and walked as swiftly as he could limp to take his leave.

Agent White was a sorry sight to behold. Both hands were bleeding, the left mangled, the right embedded with lead. His shirt was gone, and there were rope burns on his chest and arms. His back was crusted in blood, with a long cut from his shoulder blade to his lower back still dripping on and off. His pants were ripped and torn, bright red flesh showing through on his right shin where the flashbang had scalded him. The same leg was still bleeding from the puncture wound in his calf from the exploded metal door.

He was sweating, his eyes were red and swollen from the pepper spray, his ears still rang, and he kept coughing from various smokes and other fumes that had found their way into his lungs. He tried to act as natural as possible for someone without a shirt, in his condition, while limping down the sidewalk away from the building that was lit up with alarms, sirens, and arriving units, as wisps of smoke floated toward the sky. Bright search lights descended from the AP skyship that was searching the roof, and would undoubtedly soon begin to canvass the area for the escaped attackers.

The one remaining uninjured thug came running around the corner. "Agent White," he yelled, not quite angrily, more pleading. It looked like there may have been tears in his eyes. "Don't leave me here!" he begged, his voice cracking on "me." He looked even younger than before, despite the bags under his eyes, dirt on his face, and sweat-drenched clothes and body.

Agent White paused, turned to look at the boy, then turned back away without a word, and continued limping in the direction of the mag pod stop (reopened with the help of Drake). White got there, ordered a pod, and by the time it arrived seconds later, the remaining young thug was jogging up behind him, eyes wide, breathing heavy, mouth agape. White was in the pod, and the thug could see he was about to close the door.

"Just let me come with you! If they catch me they are that much closer to catching you!" he shouted, attempting anger, but sounding more like a child whose parent wouldn't get him what he wanted in the grocery store.

White sighed, like he was giving in, lazily placing his right hand in his pocket. He nodded toward the pod as if to say, "come on", and the young thug stepped forward thinking he would gain entrance and share the pod in escape. But White, in one fluid motion pulled his hand out of his pocket, aimed his handgun at the youngster's forehead, and pulled the trigger. His face was emotionless, he felt nothing. It was just easier to have no loose ends. The thug, looking more boyish than ever, crumpled to the ground dead, eyes wide, as the pod door closed.

White entered the location of a busy pod terminal in the sketchiest area he could think of, so that he could switch pods in order to elude any agents who might be following him. In the chaos it was unlikely that anyone would be on his tail anyway. He called Drake from his glasses.

Drake answered immediately, his eyes wider than normal, obviously on the edge of his seat. "Is it done?" he blurted out. "The men you sent here are dead."

"It's done. We inflicted a lot of damage on the building and equipment. It should be tough for them to run operations smoothly for a while."

"And Atlas?" Drake almost yelled it, unable to hold back.

"He's alive as far as I know."

Drake frowned, pushing his mouth to one side. He was disappointed that Atlas hadn't been taken out, but was still satisfied with the progress.

"Okay. The money is in your account." A notification presently popped up on White's glasses that confirmed the money had been deposited into an account under a false name, from an account under a false name.

Without another word, White ended the video call. Drake was left mid-sentence saying something like, "Whenever you feel up to it-."

Stepping out of the pod in the terminal, White briskly continued, walking onto the street. He ignored the stares of a few onlookers. They were no one to worry about; not the type to report that they saw him anyway. It was getting later and the area was frequented at this time mostly by drug addicts and other miscreants.

Agent White walked, still shirtless, ignoring the pain in his leg until he spotted a man with a relatively clean coat and pants. The man looked like he was coming down from some drug, and was slumped sitting against a wall at the entrance of an alleyway just off the main road, one knee bent with the foot on the ground, the other leg outstretched.

"I need your pants and jacket," White told the man in a nonchalant tone.

Looking blankly, glazed eyes lazily surveying White, the man slowly replied an unintelligible word, "whaa," that expressed confusion. White pulled a wad of notes from his pocket, rapidly counted $500 and tossed it down to the addict. The man's eyebrows raised, and his eyes widened, no doubt thinking about the next hit he would now be able to buy.

As quickly as he could, which was painfully slow and cumbersome to White, the man removed his jacket, getting caught up when it came time to slip off the second sleeve. The pants came off as he rolled onto his back, unable to keep balance, never fully standing through the whole exchange. The addict was left crouched in the alley, pantless with just a t-shirt and underwear on in the cool fall night, holding the cash in his hands, admiring it like Gollum coveting his precious ring. The last White saw of him, the man seemed to momentarily become alert, and quickly stuffed the cash into his shoe while looking around suspiciously, lest another, stronger addict take his prize.

White walked a few blocks to a different pod terminal, and entered a location on the edge of New England, close to New York City. Once there, he walked across the "border" unnoticed, and picked up yet another pod in another crowded terminal outside of the arbitrary border set by NESA. He entered a busy location on the southern west coast, and sat back, letting out a deep sigh of relief, and closing his eyes.

Less than an hour later he walked out of the pod on the west coast, and into a crowded terminal where families and businessmen stood cohorting after dinner. As Agent White slipped through the crowd, he heard bits of conversations like:

"Can you believe what's happening in New England?"

"Silly that the place where modern freedom started could be fooled so easily!"

"It's not all of them, you've got to remember the outlets reporting it have interests too."

"Those blackouts are definitely what suppressed the dissenters, we would be hearing more from them but...."

"Western Authority still has customers there, they ought to go in, guns blazing-"

"The last thing we need now is an all-out war! And there's no proof that the drug cartels *didn't* start this whole mess. Anyway why should I pay to save some idiots that got themselves into this whole mess in the first place?"

"I agree, the people of New England did this to themselves, let them deal with it!"

White pushed his way through the crowd and onto the street. Some shops would still be open so he could get better clothes. Then he'd find a place to stay. He took a deep breath of warm, sweet air. *Maybe I'll never go back* he thought.

Drake's heart was beating fast. He called in his Operations Officer.

"Give me an update on the standoffs."

"Sir all but one has been resolved. We have detained most of the Atlas Protection units opposing us, and the others have retreated and dispersed."

"Good. Let's try to get that last one under control. Inform me of any changes. Are the bodies cleaned up downstairs?"

"No sir, our team is still collecting evidence. I'll make sure we have them covered before you leave." He exited Drake's office.

Drake let out a long sigh of relief. It was working. At this point, there was no one left to stop him. Tomorrow he would do what he had to in order to finish off Atlas Protection. He would have control of what came into, and left, New England. Within a week everyone would be using NESA currency, and there would be no going back for them. Then would come the long term plan for educating the youth.

He swiveled around in his chair and stood up, looking out the window. He could see some lights in the distance on a hill. He saw an NESA skyship in the distance, floating silently over the earth. The moon was high, bright and large, almost full with the dark unlit sliver still visible in contrast to the night sky.

For a moment, Drake wondered what it was all about. Not the takeover, not power, just life. These thoughts always accompanied the sneaking memories of the girl he spent nights like these with, staring into the autumn sky, counting stars, lying on the cool damp grass, her head on his chest. He quickly pushed these thoughts from his mind. He was in the midst of the accomplishment of his lifetime, how silly to dwell on pointless episodes from the past.

Both telescreens were still on in the background. The unmuted telescreen on Economy Live caught his attention as the first news of Agent White's attack on Atlas Protection headquarters came across the screen to replace the report about the thwarted attack on NESA headquarters. He didn't turn to watch, but stared at the moon, and listened to the report delivered by a dark-skinned woman with curly hair.

"Yet another drug cartel attack has taken place, this one the boldest yet, at the same time three men violently breached NESA headquarters before being killed by the building's security. Atlas Protection Headquarters was stormed just minutes ago, by eight heavily armed men. So far we have reports of three fatalities among AP employees, as well as two employees in critical condition.

"Others are being taken to area hospitals with non-life threatening injuries including burns, smoke inhalation, and bullet wounds. As for the attackers, five are dead, one is in custody, and another has been transported to a hospital in critical condition after falling from the roof, in an attempt to repel down the side of the building. One attacker is unaccounted for.

"More details will...follow... I'm sorry I'm getting an urgent update of some breaking news. We are going to transfer you to the CEO of Independent Arbitration, addressing the public live from their headquarters."

Eleven

Drake's heart dropped and he thought he might throw up. He knew Independent Arbitration was involved in investigating the case of Barry Arbitration and Atlas Protection, inextricably linked to his takeover of New England. For them to deliver a live update at this time... *this could not be good,* Drake thought.

He whipped around to face the screen and cranked up the volume as the camera shifted to the CEO of Independent Arbitration. Drake stood, left hand supporting him on his desk, his right hand hanging limp by his side. His mouth slightly open, eyes wide, Drake watched as Independent Arbitration delivered their message.

"Good evening, my name is Odin Lancaster, CEO of Independent Arbitration. While it is not typical for our agency to release information in haste, especially while arbitration continues, the chaotic events in New England today offer extenuating circumstances. First and foremost, no concrete evidence of any actual cartel attacks having occurred in New England over the past 24 hours has been found, forwarded, or reviewed by my company. Instead, a different motive was discovered for why NESA took such criminal actions today. It starts with the case brought against Atlas Protection by Barry Arbitration.

"Independent Arbitration has found that Atlas Protection did not manufacture any evidence in the disputed case, and Barry Arbitration in fact manufactured the evidence against Atlas Protection. During the course of our investigation, Independent Arbitration found that Mr. Barry had accepted bribes, two confirmed, another still under investigation, corroborating the Business Ethics Review report released this morning."

Everyone in New England was watching or listening, and many outside as well – especially investors in New England companies. Agents in standoffs stalled their skirmishes in order to listen. If you were to float miles above New England you would have felt the region pause, breath drawn, waiting to learn their fate.

Drake stood petrified, eyes fixed on the screen, heart pounding out of his chest, mouth dry. Officer Themis watched from his hospital bed, surrounded by his family, staring intently, proud he had assisted in this release. Atlas paused for a moment from dealing with the fresh attack, and listened to the streaming broadcast from a mini-tab that someone had brought to his attention. At home, Molly stared intently at the news feed, hands clutched together like she was praying.

"Related information has also been uncovered concerning Mr. Barry's death. Two Agents were seen entering and leaving Mr. Barry's home the night of his death. An investigation has been launched into his death, to determine if it was actually a homicide. But one of the Agents who was caught on camera leaving Mr. Barry's residence was identified when he was killed invading the home of Officer James Themis last night. This Agent has contracted with New England Security Agency in the past, and there is a 67% probability according to available data, that the deceased agent has been employed by NESA within the last month.

"Everything I have told you now we know with certainty. The case is still under review, and due to the volume of employees that have been assigned to it, we expect to resolve the case quickly. While suspicion alone is not enough to convict a man in arbitration, it is enough for the public to act accordingly to protect themselves and their assets.

"It is the official position of Independent Arbitration that there is strong evidence to suggest NESA has acted, at the direction of its CEO Cole Drake, in a manner that has violated contracts with its customers, and customers of various security agencies, as well as the natural rights of men and women, without representation.

"Therefore, all warrants of NESA are hereby canceled, and any further aggressive action taken by an NESA employee will be considered an ordinary crime, without the backing of a warrant. NESA employees are urged to surrender immediately in any standoffs to avoid arbitration being brought against them. All NESA Agents must also release anyone in their captivity as a result of any warrant from the previous 36 hours, or face arbitration for false imprisonment.

"Independent Arbitration has partnered with Outside Review Arbitration to investigate and corroborate our reports, and verify their accuracy. Thank you for your time, I will now yield to the official spokesman for ORA."

"Greetings to the people of New England. Due to the explosive situation in New England over the past day, ORA has done everything in its power to expedite the process of assisting Independent Arbitration in their investigation into Barry Arbitration, New England Security Agency, the attempted murder of Molly Metis, and the home invasion, arson, and attempted murder of Officer James Themis and company. ORA vouches for the accuracy of Independent Arbitration's findings, and has issued a joint warrant, along with IA for the arrest of NESA CEO Mr. Cole Drake."

Darkness started to close in on Drake's eyes and he thought he might pass out. He stumbled back once, but caught himself, and slouched to the side into his chair. The chair swiveled slightly, so Drake was facing the side wall where his grandfather's portrait hung, stern and confident. He stared blankly at the wall in disbelief, not noticing his grandfather's gaze from the portrait, as the sound continued from the telescreen. "We urge all NESA customers to log onto OutsideReview-dot-Arbitration to connect with our representatives, and file a claim for reimbursement from NESA, and be provided with interim security."

From the window, Drake saw the men emerge from the Corner Cop Security SUV's that had been parked inconspicuously in the street, and walk toward his building's front entrance. He heard newly arriving vehicles screech to a halt in front of the building, and saw the reporters rush onto the sidewalk, waiting to catch a glimpse of Drake's arrest.

Drake briefly considered shooting himself, before ruling it out completely: he knew he wouldn't be able to do it. So he just sat in the chair, stared at the wall, and shook his head slowly from side to side, hardly a centimeter, with his head sulking down onto his chest so that his double chin looked puffier than ever, giving him a stunning resemblance to a defeated and morose blood hound.

Agents knocked on the door, then cautiously opened it, before spotting Drake, and realizing he was not a threat. Two men stood over Drake's chair and explained what was happening, though it all sounded like distant echoes to him. In a daze he got to his feet, while one of the CCS Officers lightly gripped his elbow, and the two walked him across the office, into the lobby where more Agents in business suits waited, two of whom were interviewing Drake's secretary, teary-eyed and on the edge of hysterics, acting more shocked than he probably really was at the situation.

Other employees stood around waiting for someone to tell them what to do, like they were watching their dad get arrested. A few employees actually seemed genuinely bewildered about why Drake was being arrested, but most seemed to be terrified that they would have arbitration brought against them. Some gave petrified gasps, or still clamped their hand over their mouth in disbelief.

Drake was led out to an SUV and placed in the back seat. An arbiter representing Drake met him outside, and got into the SUV with him, to advise him on the arbitration; but he knew as well as Drake that it would just be minimizing the sentence. And even then, chances were Drake would die in confinement.

CCS conducted interviews with NESA employees, and as midnight came and went security agencies resumed their normal routines, without direction or obstruction from NESA. All transportation was returned to normal, though people grumbled about how high food prices would be for the next week or so until things caught up. Early in the morning, arbiters would return to their jobs and begin the many hours of work that would have to be done, all from the past day, to sort everything out.

Arbitration was not pursued against most NESA Agents and employees; a few with more information, like the Agent who led the raid on Coastal Internet, and Drake's secretary, Benjamin, were forced to pay restitution to victims. As for those people and companies involved in helping NESA, the market cleared them out like dead brush in a wildfire.

Mr. Patrick of Minutemen Arms tried to stay afloat, though after a few days of being hounded by the media and his customers, the board finally removed him as CEO. Stocks had plummeted over 50% and MA lost almost a quarter of its customers within a week, since rumors started swirling of Patrick's involvement in the takeover, due to his early support of Drake. Criminal investigations would dog Patrick for the better part of a year, until he was finally arrested, attempting to flee New England, and charged with criminal coercion in practicing his capacity as Minister of Transportation. He was confined for five years and fined heavily, but his vast fortune could take the hit. Most of his sentence was served on his own property, playing tennis, swimming in his pool, and throwing parties. He would emerge a shamed alcoholic, shunned by most, except his elitist friends who cared more about money than integrity.

Coastal Internet was downgraded by BER for its CEO's submission to Drake's Agents, but the criminal investigation could find no concrete evidence against the CEO. He resigned in an attempt to keep the company profitable, but it was to no avail. Coastal Internet went under, and its assets were auctioned off. Some 30 former employees, who had been detained by NESA Agents at Coastal Internet, bought back most of the company, and started their own Internet provider called Open Internet. They decentralized the offices, and added blockers to assure that their customers could not simply have the plug pulled on their services again. The company thrived.

As part of the arbitration arrangement, Drake was forced to sell his 55% stake in News of New England, which was bought up by two smaller but growing news organizations, one of which helped call out the inconsistencies in NESA's story the day of the takeover, establishing their reputation. The rest of NNE was bought by Business Ethics Review which expanded their business model, and News of New England ceased to exist as a media company.

Those Ministers who had signed onto Drake's plan, but not actively engaged in the takeover, escaped arbitration, but could not thwart the public backlash. They all lost their prominent jobs in shame, two fleeing to different parts of the world, their wallets a little lighter due to some civil settlements. One killed himself when his wife left him and took their kids, his house, and most of his bank accounts. Another moved into an adap after becoming destitute, apparently not realizing that the money in her bank would not last forever. She became well known as the seedy part of town's resident drunk.

The CEO of Collective Arbitration was arrested on a Caribbean island two months after the attempted takeover, and extradited to New England to face arbitration. He stood accused by his Board of soliciting a bribe, and accused by customers of various agencies of breaches of contract for undermining contracts and issuing false warrants without evidence. He settled mostly by paying fines, spent 6 months confined to adap house arrest, and then returned to Cuba, living out his life substantially more frugally than he was used to. Collective Arbitration went out of business before the CEO was even released from his adap confinement.

Collective Arbitration's assets and accounts were bought at a steep discount by Molly Metis. She had received awards, and became relatively famous for her heroism and courage in journalism, in the face of dire consequences, and threats to her life. She started Metis Arbitration, and due to her reputation, had no trouble finding financial backers and clients. The agency thrived, and would eventually become one of the largest and most respected arbitration agencies in New England.

Atlas Protection was an early customer of Metis Arbitration. Atlas had gained back all of its customers that had been lost due to the defamation from Barry Arbitration and NESA, plus another half million. AP had also found a skilled director for their new street divisions: Officer Themis – rather Director Themis. He left Corner Cop Security, disappointed that they caved so easily to the demands of NESA during the crisis.

Drake was confined to an adap after all his assets were sold off to pay restitution to some of his victims, including the families of the slain Atlas Protection employees. Sentenced to 60 years in confinement, Drake died of a heart attack in his adap six years later. That last year, Mr. Patrick never went to visit him, despite Mr. Drake's requests.

One year after Drake's attack on New England; Molly Metis, Kitt Atlas, and James Themis met for dinner in a basement bistro, which was not unusual as they had become quite close friends in the process of keeping New England free from the shackles of Drake's would-be government. They joked that meetings like these were executive dinners, for business only, while in reality work could not be further from their minds when the three friends met for leisure.

"Do you know what today is?" Atlas asked his companions as he poured himself another glass of sparkling wine, the previous jovial laughter dying down.

"Did I forget your birthday?" Molly asked finishing her glass, and reaching once more for the bottle, then filling up Themis's glass to a thank-you nod from him.

"No, no," Atlas laughed. "Today is the one year anniversary since we saved New England from tyranny!"

The three burst out laughing, taking it as a joke... even though they more or less *had* singlehandedly saved New England. The laughter could have been partly the sparkling wine's influence as well.

"You know I'll never understand it," Molly said shaking her head. "Drake had everything he needed, everything he could have ever wanted. Why would he give it all up for such a stupid reason?"

Atlas let out a laugh, but then reeled it in apologetically. "Sorry," he said, "but you guys are young. These days there's only so much power to be had, right? Money gets you power, but still it's a different type of power. And yeah, you could *buy* power back in the days before the collapse, but now there's no one to buy it *from*. Today you get power only if you provide people with something they want. You used to just be able to take it from them by force. That's what Drake was trying to resurrect.

"I guess what I am saying is, there's no going back for these guys – Drake and Barry types; if their wallet shrinks, their power shrinks. Power will make people do some crazy things, and, well... you get used to a lifestyle quickly. The bank has got to keep swelling or they'll feel irrelevant and worthless. Money, the market, customers – that's the only way to do it these days. You can't just force people to respect you. You can't just buy a share of the market like you used to be able to from government. You gotta earn it, to put in the time, the effort, and work for it. He was trying to skirt the system, hold onto something his father and grandfather created, but he couldn't sustain."

Themis nodded in agreement, Molly shrugged in agreement.

"So I suggest a toast," Atlas continued, "To friendship, truth, and freedom. To Molly's thriving new business, and AP's outstanding new Director. To New England, and indeed the world, and the sovereignty of each and every one of her inhabitants. To the hope that the earth's transformation to a world free of slavery soon be complete. To future generations, that they recognize the gift of being born free, and never squander that opportunity. That we never become complacent, and put more value in ease than equality. Uh let's see... did I miss anything?"

"To Mr. Atlas!" Molly joyfully interjected, raising her glass, "That he live long, and continue to prosper, as a reward for the risk he took to keep a free people free. And to Director Themis! That his quality of life may match the quality of his commitment to standing guard for the natural rights of every man, woman, and child!"

"And to Ms. Molly Metis!" Themis piped in, "For overcoming the odds against murderers and thieves, and standing strong in the face of the worst adversity, to bring truth to the people of New England, whether they wanted to hear it or not!"

The three heartily raised their glasses toward the ceiling, clinked them together, and downed the contents, before continuing their revelry.

There was order and peace, wealth and happiness, freedom and equality. The region was secure. There was still anarchy in New England.

ABOUT THE AUTHOR

Joe Jarvis was born in 1989 in suburban Massachusetts, and along with two older sisters, was raised by two loving parents. He considers Ayn Rand a major influence, having devoured her non-fiction Objectivist writings as well as the fiction classics *Atlas Shrugged*, and *The Fountainhead*. Joe aspires to pick up where Rand left off in a sense, but hopes to appeal to a larger audience with less preaching, and more consistency in bringing the non-aggression principle to its logical conclusion: eliminating government altogether. After the 2012 start of his political blog, JoeJarvis.me, his disillusion with government accelerated with every bit of research. Later he started a more lighthearted philosophical blog, JoeJarvisExplainsItAll.com, in order to move away from strictly political issues, and keep himself sane. Joe aspires to spread his knowledge and views of a better future through fiction, including what he considers to be his first of many, ***Anarchy in New England***.